for my baby JUNE .

New York City

Beast

Coming of Age in the Boroughs
1984-1994

By
Chris Anthony

Paperback Edition November 2024

CONTACT – INSTAGRAM
@bronxscienceog
allstreetofficial@gmail.com

ISBN: 979-8-89587-759-3

CMLLC ENTERTAINMENT
11333 MOORPARK STREET 392
STUDIO CITY, CA 91602

Imagine how boring life would be if we all did only what we were supposed to do.

Thank you for being you.

TABLE OF CONTENTS

INTRODUCTION

I want to be uncomfortable.

Maybe I don't really want to, but I have to. I spent too many years outside of New York in a comfortable position and it was a complete vacuum where nothing worthwhile happened. The more comfortable I got, the less I did. And as an artist that is absolute death, nothing is worse for art than comfort.

When I was writing my previous book to this one, (New York City Prose) my wife saw that I was writing every day for months with a dedication she hadn't seen in years.

Yet I wasn't working professionally as a writer, I wasn't working at all. I pretty much got cancelled from society by my age and overqualifications during the pandemic and had been unemployed for the most part of the past three years at the time. Having had a few successful ventures prior to that, I was in a position where I could kiss the working world goodbye forever. I was not rich, but my side hustles and what I had were enough that I could foreseeably still provide for myself and family and cover my share of the bills for many years to come, and that made me comfortable.

It wasn't the first time I was comfortable; I had done well before and mismanaged my life and wound up back at zero and had to do it over again. It was a pattern in my life. Obviously stemming from my youth where my decisions were not always thought out properly before I'd acted.

Unfortunately, this time was no different, I'd spent too much money too fast and wound up in a situation where it was back to the proverbial drawing board. I needed to give up the comfort I enjoyed for 2020 and 2021 and move out of our luxurious house and move the family into an apartment in a not so nice area, a byproduct of which would eliminate my comfort. Not by design but by necessity.

Which we did, and for sure part of that decision was impacted by my realization that I was once again living in a vacuum, disconnected from reality. I was focusing on things that weren't me and focusing on things that weren't my art, in any way. In my life, I have always been my art.

So, when my wife saw that I was writing she asked what I was doing, and I told her "Writing one of the first of many volumes of my story," I said.

"You're actual story? Why would you do that, what is your motivation for this again?"

She went on to ask if she could read some of it and she did and after the first 10 pages she complained that it was far too much, and she was totally uncomfortable with me doing this. And that's how I knew I was doing the right thing. Because art is never created from a place of comfort, nor is it meant to make people feel comfortable. That previous book did go through a solid couple of months of just editing, eventually taming it down to what I felt was acceptable to my own motivations and to get it to a place where I felt proud of the work.

Sure, some artists do have an easier path, sometimes great artists get "discovered" early on in their careers by someone influential or wealthy that is emotionally moved by their art in some way and that someone has the means or connections to propel them to stardom. That does happen and in that instance the artist may not have remained uncomfortable for long, and sometimes that hurts their new work once they have all their newfound money and means. It happens many times with musical artists where their debut album is so unbelievable, but each subsequent album gets worse and worse as their success continues.

Sometimes even awful artists get lucky, but that's rare. Far more common however, is many amazing and talented artists never make a living doing their work, especially while they are alive. And in some ways that is best artwork of all, because that art always comes from a place of discomfort and the artist was able to express that discomfort in a way that made the beholder uncomfortable or at least feel something, even if it was pleasurable. And it's that cause and effect that makes the experience of art what it is. You have to feel something.

As artists growing up and kids living in NYC during the crazy 1980s, my previous book dealt with a lot of the motivations we had as kids to do the things we did and express ourselves the way we did. And I started to touch on it a bit in some stories and towards the end when I talked about redemption from the perspective of now looking back. Since then, I have continued to reflect and have thoughts about how our childhood angst and missteps, deliberate or not, shaped us as human beings and connected to us as people as we got older.

Who did we become?

Even in theory, with all the violence and darkness we lived through, what was the result of mixing that violence and darkness directly with our pleasure centers in our brains as we were finding fun or enjoyment amidst the madness? Surely there had to be some lasting effect to the humans we developed into.

My Bronx High School of Science yearbook photo is here -

Incorporating a lyric from a punk rock anthem into my yearbook and adding my own "Hope", I subtly signaled a deep-seated wish for absolution and understanding from the person I'd eventually become. At 16, how could I have foreseen this quest for self-forgiveness? I cheekily challenged everyone at school with that thought, eschewing the expected inspirational maxim for a reflective provocation.

I was driven by a curiosity about the future's perspective on my own choices—pondering whether they'd be subjects of regret or humorous anecdotes.

I sensed the inevitability of consequences, a lingering aftermath from the paths I chose.

As with my previous volume, this book will inevitably leave untold tales in its wake, stories that this book won't capture, not for lack of significance but more so due to timing or readiness. Some narratives remain just out of reach to me currently, embarrassing or maybe too harsh. I'm awaiting a moment when I'm ready to share them, understanding that each story, told or untold, shapes the continuum of my journey until I, like all of us, move on from this existence into the next. Or lack thereof, however unfortunate the final result will be for all of us.

If you read my previous book, you might read a few lines here and there and think to yourself that I already said that in the first book. It won't happen often but in order that this book stands on its own it is sometimes necessary to briefly recount an idea or two.
As you read these stories, think of your own coming of age tales. How do you feel about who you are as it relates to who you were as a youth?

I look back fondly, with a sense of nostalgia that is painful. Not out of a loathing for my current life but more so a loathing for adulthood in general, a cliché theme that it sucks to grow up. But I honestly feel it's much more than that for some of us.

There is a darkness to life and those of us that have connected with the darkest parts of the human desire and found pleasure in such growing up miss that ability to be ourselves. As fucked up as it was, there was always something so joyfully sinister to being out in the city late at night when most normal citizens were locked safely in their homes asleep. Throwing caution to the wind in a way that reflected how little caution there was to begin with. The crimes we committed, the violence of which we became part, the hype of it all was a barbaric drug that addicted many of us to the core. The city itself was a drug that is hard to quit, and as most addicts with addictions they have put aside for the betterment of their own lives, the longing for that taste never truly goes away.

I chose the title because I still grapple with this thought today, was it us or the environment? Or maybe there was and is a beast just waiting to get a hold of us if we let it.

Bayside had a nightlife scene that erupted in about 1988, even city kids from Manhattan and Brooklyn would start hanging out there.
But in 1990 I got out, I went away to college in Arizona, sight unseen. I had never even been west of New Jersey, but I knew I wanted to get as far away from Bayside as possible by then. New York City life was fun, but it was also hard.

That should have been my Once upon a time moment for New York. Except that on a winter break in 1991 from college, I would get arrested and charged with a crime serious enough that I couldn't leave the state. I had to drop out of college to clear it up.

I had to move back to Queens in 1991 and with that began my second story in New York, it was now Twice Upon a Time in Queens. And as hard as it is to believe, the second time around went as outrageously insane as the first.

Some of the stories here predate my original escape from Bayside, some afterward, either way, it feels I have lived more than one life in New York City and Queens.

If you read my last book, you know how it goes. Some names have been changed, some locations. Most of it is left unchanged, some liberties were taken in the interest of art. But most of it really happened, in some way, even if mostly as perceived by me as a youth living through it. Some of the crimes discussed are complete fantasy.

But if you really think about it, isn't life just a fantasy to begin with? Gone as quickly as it started.

CHAPTER 1

MAJOR CHAOS

In 1979 I was just getting out of a lengthy treatment in a children's hospital. I was in the 4th grade and by now I did attend school with the other kids and my brother. In the years prior I would miss about one week each month being treated for a terminal illness, initially diagnosed as Leukemia in 1972.

The specifics of my health struggles aren't the focus of my story, but they did impact how I socialized during my early years, particularly when it came to the whole boy-girl dynamic. This set the stage for some awkward teenage years, especially around girls, since those were my first real attempts at such interactions. My growth was also notably delayed for a while. Surprising both to the doctors and my parents, I experienced a growth spurt in my late teens. By the time I turned 21, I had reached 6 feet tall. At 18, though, I was still catching up; I was about 5 foot 9 inches tall, weighed around 125 pounds, and still had the youthful look of a 12-year-old.

Another byproduct of my early childhood in the children's hospital is I was sick, so sick that it was dangerous for me to participate in any physical activity, and I was rarely allowed to play outside with my brother and the other kids until I was 9 years old. At this time, they removed my diseased spleen and managed to send my condition into what was thought of as a remission. So, when I got out, it was like getting out of jail in a sense, I was being introduced to a society I knew nothing about, socially, and activity wise, and I went a little crazy I think to make up for lost time.

That same year our Catholic school set up a computer lab, something extremely rare in 1979, for most schools, and anywhere for that matter. The personal computer was a brand-new concept only a year or two old at that point and our school Sacred Heart purchased two "Commodore PET" computers. A monolithic thing with keyboard and monitor all built into the same shell boasting a powerful 24K or about that, of built in RAM memory. Imagine that?

I'm not sure what it took to participate in that lab, but my brother and I did. It may have just been there was no other interest from many of the students because it was a foreign concept, or maybe because we were a little bit on the nerdy side the school invited us. I can't remember.

Either way, we excelled in there, catching on quickly and my parents noticed this and the following Christmas in 1980 bought us an Atari 800 personal computer, with a modem and a floppy drive. All things we requested and understood at the age of not even 10 yet.

Strange parallel here with this new world of computing and the graffiti world which would start for us soon after. It didn't take long for us to reach the dark side of this either. A pattern in our childhoods that repeated through everything we participated in. Was it just us? Or was this indicative of the time and period in history?

In "Lord of the Flies," they contemplate whether a beast truly existed or if the darkness emerged from within themselves. I think human nature is inherently prone to establishing hierarchies and succumbing to savagery in the absence of societal constraints.

Similarly, the characters of that story were marooned on an island, and in many ways, we too found ourselves isolated, marooned so to speak, in 1970s and 1980s New York City. Economic hard and dark times making the city equal parts scary and fantastic. Does the beast thrive on this kind of vulnerability, waiting to exploit the darker facets of human nature and the world?

It's likely that the monster is us, though I'm not ready to commit to that thought. I begin this book with this story of us and computers to underscore our own entanglement with the crimes and misdemeanors they helped facilitate. Our parents gifted us a computer intended for home use at a time when outside data connections were almost nonexistent and unheard of by the masses. But this seemingly benign gift led us to a sinister underbelly, culminating in real-world violence and crime, all facilitated by the very same technology. Yet, it remains ambiguous whether the beast was real or merely a reflection of ourselves.

Graffiti clearly links to criminal behavior, driven by a mix of parental neglect, economic hardship, boredom, and the challenges of urban life. However, our experience with computers presents a different narrative. It wasn't inherently malevolent, yet we stumbled upon or were perhaps lured into its dark realms. Realms that we associate with a dark side of the web today, but the truth is, that dark side existed analogous to the advent of computers, furthering the evidence that mankind will always find a way. We always did find a way.

I'll delve deeper into these thoughts towards the book's conclusion. For now, follow this wild story from one chapter to the next and form your own judgments.

DISK OPERATING SYSTEM

A little bit about the interface of computers back then to note. It is completely removed from today's world of User Interface (UI) and User Experience (UX). There was nothing on a computer when you turned it on. Nothing in memory, only its bare machine language code, hidden behind a cursor awaiting a prompt of some kind. There was technically a mechanical user interface but graphically nothing there.

That's all you would see, a blank screen with a flashing single cursor that appeared in the top left. It was very mysterious and such a departure from today's Windows or MacOS that immediately greets you and walks you through an interaction of some kind.

By 1980 Microsoft was already a thing, Bill Gates was already a thing and Steve Jobs was already a thing although Bill Gates and Microsoft were off to an early domination. Almost all computers at that time functioned on Microsoft DOS prompts, MS_DOS as it was known. Of course, the MS in that name was proprietary to Microsoft and limited to the IBM machines or clones that worked with Microsoft, but each brand would have its own spin off DOS, like the Atari had "Atari DOS" and so on. It was similar.

DOS stood for "Disk Operating System" which says it all right there. For the most part, when you turned on your computer, you would prompt the computer to access a drive or some ROM (Read Only Memory) attachment of some sort, like a cartridge plug in.

The command prompts we entered with the keyboard look similar to directory prompts on Windows machines today - "/:drive1-open" or some jargon like that, and it would access a disk and print in plain keyboard characters a catalogue or inventory right beneath your prompt. All in the same screen, there were no windows or other screen views at this time. It all happened in linear fashion from top to bottom and scrolled down when the screen was full.

Computers oddly enough came with books. There was no "Looking something up" on the computer at this time. If you needed to look something up that would be in a book. Otherwise, you went in dark and figured it out as you went.

From the drive prompt or command the computer would access the external drive, everything was external, and return a list or catalogue after a series of audible buzzes and clicks. You would select something from this list by typing another cryptic prompt. There was also no mouse or anyway to move the cursor around beyond the keyboard which may or may not even have usable arrow keys to navigate yet. Often, you might be loading in a compiler language or interface which would then let you code in "Basic" or "Pascal", "Fortran", "Assembly" etc. and that program would compile and run your coding in the base machine language of the device. Which is what is commonly referred to as Binary, ones and zeros, each not representing a number as much as 1 being a switch on and 0 being a switch off.

It is not my intent to get into a verifiable lesson on how to code and run computers back then, I'm going completely by 40 years' worth of memory here. I am probably a little loose with some of the terminology, but I am close enough, certainly for this book.

If you're around 40, you probably remember dial-up modems with AOL. Many were dialing into mainframe databases, a precursor to the internet. But just before that, in my generation of tech (about 10-

year increments), we used acoustic modems with rotary phones. You'd dial a number, then jam the phone's handset into suction cups on the modem to send and receive tones. It wasn't far from two cans and a string.

Soon we upgraded to digital modems like the MPC 3000, thanks to push-button phones. Early online connections were often just dialing another person's computer—one user at a time. Unless you had multiple phone lines, you'd hear a busy signal for hours.

BBS (Bulletin Board Systems) were mostly run by teens and hackers. These systems shared pirated software, illegal codes, and more. Downloading a 48K game took maybe 15 minutes, byte by byte. Long-distance calls to other systems were expensive, so we hacked calling card numbers or used tricks like "Phreaking" with black boxes to bypass phone charges.

Hacking wasn't just for fun—it was currency. We traded pirated software, calling codes, and BBS advertisements in exchange for access. The floppy disks we used were truly floppy, unlike the rigid 3.5" disks that came later.

Text-based games, similar to Dungeons & Dragons, were common. You'd program adventure modules and let players choose outcomes. This concept of interactive storytelling is coming back with things like Netflix's choose-your-adventure shows.

Running a BBS made you the SYSOP, or system operator. BBS users could chat with the SYSOP through a feature that rang a bell on your computer. Occasionally, someone would type "Go voice," meaning you'd both pick up the phone simultaneously switching off the modem for a real-world conversation. This was especially nerve-wracking for 10-year-olds like us, running a pirate BBS. You never wanted them to realize that we were kids!

GONE CATFISHING

People tend to think "Catfishing" is a new phenomenon that came along with creating online identities on dating apps and social media, but the concept of pretending to be someone else has always existed in human nature, way back into the Dark Ages and even before.

And it is no surprise that being catfished became an immediate thing as soon as we got online with computers and grew from there. I mentioned above that we were hiding the fact that we were 10-year old's by not wanting to ever "Go voice" in a chat situation, and others were hiding the fact that they were 40-year-olds in the same manner. Some were hiding their gender or some other proclivity, nefarious or otherwise. In general, it was common for people to be hiding behind some false premise then, just as it is now.

There was a BBS called Vortex and the SYSOP name was "View" and he claimed to be 11 years old. My brother used to regularly try to get him to go voice to discuss the trade of a game View claimed on his BBS to have in his possession. One morning Jimmy, yes, the same Jimmy Tame from my first book and future graffiti days, came into our room before school and was looking at some printouts and saw something from Vortex on there.

"Did you ever speak to that guy?" he said to my brother.

"Nah, he's in a wheelchair," my brother responded for some reason as we all started laughing. Not at the fact that he was in a wheelchair, but at the fact that my brother thought that was a reason the guy couldn't speak.

My brother asked him one time to "Go voice" and he said he couldn't and in my brother's mind he thought there was something wrong with the guy in some way and then eventually just assumed he was in a wheelchair and couldn't speak, like Stephen Hawking.

But we found out later after a larger incident that the guy was older and was doing creepy shit interacting with kids online. A version of this story is the basis for a screenplay I wrote and had in production and am rewriting and maybe trying to move it forward again now.

Tapper –

A new game was released with modern, at the time security features. It was a little tough to crack but was also selling for like $20 which meant we couldn't even get a copy to crack it.
But it was a hot item and everyone in the piracy circle wanted it, so we had to have it.

Through trades and various favors and interactions with others on their BBSs you could be granted privileges that ranged in security levels, the highest being SYSOP Privileges.

This highest level of security would be reserved for people you really trusted and in most cases people you really knew.

My brother had formed a few bonds however and at a BBS called WARTIME, my brother had achieved a high level of security similar, or very close to it. With this level of access, you could damage someone's BBS and files and delete disks, etc, so it was usually not taken lightly, and it was rare for someone you never met in real life to get this kind of unfettered control.

Mistakenly the SYSOP of WARTIME had left the videogame Tapper in a drive that my brother could access, almost the very day he cracked it, and it was brand new. My brother was on his BBS and saw it in his drive and knew it wasn't supposed to be there, but my brother downloaded it anyway.

The next day when Jimmy was over again, the SYSOP of WARTIME, a 15-year-old kid who went by the handle "Major Chaos" realized my brother took it and was furious because he wanted something in a trade for it since it was so hard to get, and he was frantically hitting the "Chat SYSOP" button on our BBS. My brother knew he fucked up by taking it and didn't want to speak to him. Jimmy got on the keyboard and responded as my brother and Major Chaos demanded he "Go Voice!!!"

Not knowing what to do Jimmy picked up and spoke to the kid who we could hear screaming through the telephone. Jimmy covered the mouse piece and said he was demanding 2 boxes of floppy disks for it, which would have cost almost the price of the game at retail. We refused but negotiated it down to one box and set up a meeting in Crocheron Park for the next day at 3pm after school.

This was a huge thing for us at the time. We had never met anyone in real life from the computer world. It was hard enough for us to go voice in the first place. Now this older kid was coming with another kid "The General" to collect on this debt and we were kind of scared about what was going to happen. To this day I remember the description someone gave us when we asked about the General, it wasn't very nice but was funny. They described him as a "Fat nerd with glasses."

Our friend Gibson was always playing roller hockey at this point and was always on roller skates. That is such a typical thing back then that you would never see today. A kid leaving his house on roller skates and not even bringing sneakers.

We told Gibson what was going on and he agreed to come with us. He was bringing a baseball bat just in case. To make clear the optics of this, Gibson, if you hadn't read my first book is a black kid and one year older than us, he was in fairly good shape and strong. The other three of us, my brother, Jimmy were white, with me looking somewhat Asian for some reason. The two kids we were going to meet were Jewish from Bay Terrace.

Bayside was segregated enough at the time that we had never met many Jewish kids yet, being in Catholic School. And most kids from Bay Terrace had never met a black kid yet, or at least not many.

When we got to Crocheron park we could see Major Chaos and The General standing next to their bikes. We originally told Gibson to hang back a little until we saw what was going on with them because they were only expecting me, my brother and Jimmy.

Major Chaos had a pair of Nun Chucks in his hands, which was a martial arts weapon for those not familiar with the term. Gibson saw this and came skating up with the baseball bat in his hand.

Major Chaos and The General panicked because now Gibson was skating towards them with a baseball bat, Major Chaos threw down his weapon and they jumped on their bicycles and peddled as fast as they could away from us. Gibson for some reason kept skating after them and we started running along with him.

The path they were headed down in the park turns into a concrete staircase without much warning, it could be dangerous if you didn't know the park, and they didn't.

Major Chaos went down the stairs on his bicycle and tumbled to the bottom knocking out his front teeth and injuring himself badly. We watched the aftermath of the accident, and the General was screaming for help. Major Chaos lay at the bottom of the steps in a heap, a broken, bloody mess.

People from the park came over and an ambulance arrived, and we left. We felt bad for the kid but saw it as it was his fault in the first place. First, he showed up with a weapon, second, they were trying to bully us a bit anyway being almost 4 years older than us and all.

A few days later my brother was wondering what became of the situation. He called to log on to

WARTIME BBS to speak with Major Chaos, but the phone just rang and rang.

My brother kept trying the whole afternoon before a woman answered. It was Major Chaos's mother. Turns out her kid had to stay in the hospital overnight with a concussion and was badly bruised up and needed dental work. The BBS was down indefinitely.

The next day Jimmy's brother Michael heard what happened and insisted we go over to this kid's house to see him and make sure he is alright. We called again and made arrangements with his mom and did. We walked into a Bay Terrace apartment building later that day and visited a kid we never met in his bed all bandaged up.

It was as awkward as you might imagine. There is a bit more to this story and turns out Major Chaos was actually a girl which we never even realized in the first place. But that's what the movie is about. If it comes out, go see it. If not, I suppose I will make that entire story a book in another year or so.

CHAPTER 2

INKFAST SCARECROW

My brother who went on to write DROMA as a graffiti tag, often says that he started writing graffiti before I did, and in many ways, at least locally, he is correct.

Around this same time in 1982 as the computers and associated chaos, he came up with a graffiti tag SCARECROW and was doing drippy marker tags up and down Bell Boulevard with our friend Alex Rowens who was writing INK FAST.

They hit up stairwells and business bathrooms and the local YMCA building and did manage to get some ups at the time. It was always written INK FAST first then the marker handed to my brother to write SCARECROW and for a moment they were known as exactly that. Inkfast Scarecrow. Man... what I would do for pictures of their tags now.

Gibson started to write with them a bit using the tag GIB and they would all go racking for supplies together, although Gibson would never steal. One day he was pressured into stealing a box of markers from an art store on Bell Boulevard named Kurtzberg's and he did.

The next day he was so overridden with guilt that he went back to the store and told them what he did and paid for the box of markers. They commended him on his character while we simultaneous laughed at him and teased him for being soft.

I did have a tag in 1982 along with them but did not ever go bombing really except a couple of tags at the park house and tennis courts. My tag was CEE-MINO, and I would stay focused more on breakdancing at the time than graffiti. By 1983 computers were still a part of our lives but not the main focus anymore. We were breakdancing and Skating and riding BMX more, and I was also starting Bronx High School of Science that year at 12 years old. Which was young.

My going to Bronx High School of Science was supposed to further my interests in computers, math and science, already being fascinated by the three and well above my grade level in all subjects.

But ironically it introduced me to the streets and pushed me further into graffiti. Riding the subway to high school exposed me to the New York City part of graffiti above the local level and drew me in.

THE WHALE'S STOMACH

Breakdancing was wildly popular by 1982 with television specials, commercials, and movies and for a minute, it seemed like the world to us. It was tied closely, at least by the media, to hip hop and graffiti which we were already into a bit. All of the hype around graffiti as it related to breakdancing in the media definitely led to a broader interest in graffiti for us. And in Bayside Queens break dancing meant one of two things, USA (United Skates of America) in Jackson Heights-ish area under the 7 Line, or Laces Skating rink in Lake Success or somewhere around there. You might remember USA Skates if you read my first book as the club under the elevated station that led to a fight we got into in late 1986 or early 1987.

I only started riding the 7 train for Bronx Science daily in 1983 so prior to then that wasn't as common for us. Most kids in eastern Queens went to Laces. It was more convenient and a little bit of a softer crowd.

USA had clubs and gangs like the Ballbusters, Decepticons and others associated with the area which was a little bit intimidating to us. (Incidentally, when I type the names of some of these groups, I feel like I made them up, I didn't, but it's been so long I may have gotten some of the names in this book wrong.)

Laces had two rinks inside, one main rink and a second smaller rink. With the popularity of breaking at this time, Thursday, Friday, and Saturday would have that smaller rink dedicated to breaking. You would not rent skates but instead put on your flyest (Dopest, nicest, etc.) B-Boy or B-Girl attire and head into that rink with a crowd of others cheering and dancing to the breakdancing music of the time. Often circles of people would form where battles or people would jump in one after another and perform their latest moves and acrobatics to the cheers or boos of the crowd. Often there were actual boos, that was the point, you were judged to have won or lost by the crowd reaction, like the way hip hop events and battles were traditionally judged.

I had one signature move which at the time was pretty advanced. I did head windmills barely but could get about 4 decent ones quickly before I started to fall apart, it used to be that I would fizzle out here into a lame backspin or something with almost no reaction from the crowd. But I developed what was later known as an air track, a head windmill where you do a rep or two without any part of your body touching the floor, sort of almost like a head spin but still with your body more horizontal and using the windmill momentum and your hands.

That fantastic ending into a bridge freeze at the end or a backspin pop up to airborne and out would get me some cheers from time to time. For a couple of weeks anyway before others learned to do it and it quickly became run of the mill.

Fights would break out at Laces too, but far less than at USA in Jackson Heights, another reason we preferred this location, it was closer to home and safer.

In the very early days of breakdancing, for each of us and the activity in general, we used flattened cardboard boxes. People would put cardboard on street corners to perform. It created a slippery-ish surface that you could spin on and would protect you from abrasions caused by the concrete or hard surfaces.

Another upside to performing on cardboard would be that after the performance, wherever you were you could just throw it in the trash and get more for next time.

But as you took breakdancing more seriously you would save up money or pool money with your friends, or steal, and have someone drive you to a local flooring supplier or lumber yard. Something like Pergament, or Sears and you would buy an 6x8 or so piece of linoleum and roll it up taking it home.

You could also roll it for transport to perform outside of your house, and we would roll it often. Linoleum could also be set on a street corner to perform but unlike the cardboard you would not throw it away when you were done. You would roll it up at the end and take it back with you.

All this rolling created another crazy thing we used to do, something my brother called "The Whale's Stomach".

We were in Catholic school and had learned about Jonah, someone that pissed off God in some way and was swallowed up by a whale and forced to atone for their sins inside the belly of the whale. The school taught this to us as if it actually happened and this person lived three days in a whale's stomach. Something we found absurd.

Without even stating an opinion on Catholicism or any religion at all, I understand those stories to be parables, fables designed to teach a lesson and not actual events. But there are some that believe things like that were an actual event which is what led to our pondering and discussions as young kids.

***I feel the need to preface this next part with a note, yes what you are about to read happened and yes it was an awful idea. Do not under any circumstances attempt this.

There was this challenge between my brother and a local kid named Tuff Tommy. Well, that wasn't really his name, it was like Tom Tufiano or some shit but after this night we would change it to the former.

It was common for us to roll each other up in the linoleum which was like being buried alive. Just penning this story now is making my skin crawl. It was the worst feeling, we would roll someone up and then scream down into the end of the tube to see if you were ok, and no one ever was, almost everyone that ever made it to this point was shrieking bloody murder and we would unroll them as quickly as we rolled them in the first place.

Those of us that could bring ourselves to this point without screaming would then be put in the whale's stomach. This sounds like the narrative of a horror movie in writing, but this really happened and was something we did often.

Some of us would build up a comfort level with the original rolling, figuring that if we angled our heads upward just enough, we could see light and know we would always have air. But this next part was so sinister.

The whale's stomach meant that one of us would fold over the top of the tube and another would fold over the bottom of the tube. Essentially burying alive the person that was inside.

It was rolled so tightly that you could not even budge your arms and once the whale's stomach was applied, we could barely even hear the shrieks of those inside. We were not stupid however, despite our age, and would always unwrap the person within a strict few seconds so as not to suffocate anyone.

This game led to several children running from my house in tears and trauma never to return. Even I have a long-term fear of confined spaces now.

Tuff Tommy was talking a lot of shit that he could do the whale's stomach and that he wasn't afraid. Something my brother took as gibberish and insisted it would break him immediately.

To make matters worse, Jimmy Tame had sustained a kidney injury as a child and only had one kidney, he had this elastic belt he was supposed to wear around his midsection when he played sports. Sometimes for an added bit of torture we would tie someone's arms at their side with the kidney belt before rolling them up, just layer upon layer of complete helplessness.

Tommy insisted we do this too. First time he was ever doing this on this fateful day. He just saw another kid come out hysterical crying, he mocked the kid. The kid cried "but I couldn't breathe", and Tommy responded "But you could have held your breath for longer than 2 seconds, right? Pussy!"

My brother wrapped up Tommy's arms. "Don't let me out for at least two minutes" Tommy says. "Yeah right," my brother responds.

We rolled him up and announced into the tube that here comes the whale's stomach before folding him up.

Now I don't know if you are familiar with a minute when it comes to holding your breath, especially above water. It feels like forever. Probably about 15 seconds went by before Jimmy yells, "Ok let him out of there!"

My brother looking closely at a watch tells Jimmy its only be 20 seconds, and they start arguing, Jimmy undoes the end of the tube and asks Tommy if he's alright. We hear a muffled voice "What'd you open it for!" exclaims Tommy. "It hasn't been even close to a minute yet."

We fold him back up. We count down to another minute which felt like an eternity and yell to him, but there is no response. In a panic we frantically unroll the tube and he lay there still. Unconscious or dead. What the fuck?

No one says anything, one kid in the room burst into tears causing Tommy to open his eyes because he was faking. "You guys are fucking losers." He said.

From that moment forward he was known as Tuff Tommy. I still stand by this till today, anyone that thinks they could brave the whale's stomach is wrong. Tommy was one of a kind and I'm certain it would still break almost anyone. Although I would never suggest anyone try.

UNDERGROUND BOXING

My dad bought me and my brother a set of boxing gloves each and headgear. He was a huge fight fan and a boxer in the Marines and used to try to teach us to box and hoped we would box each other.

I think my dad was so excited that I was no longer hospitalized, and it was now safe for me to be physical that he wanted to push me into as much physicality as possible. He also worried that I used to be bullied a little bit by one of my brother's friends and he would see it when they came to the house.

My dad used to insist that I don't take that shit from him or anyone and egged me on to stand up to myself which rarely happened in the beginning, I was just too small and too weak, mentally and physically.

My brother wanted nothing to do with the boxing gear so his remained essentially brand new. My dad would get on his knees and box me just holding my brothers' gloves in each hand without putting them on, giving me little light jabs and parrying my punches. As I said, he was a wartime Marine soldier; he knew a lot about fighting and boxing and trained me a bit when I was about 10 or 11 years old.

Eventually I got better, and he grew tired of me punching him in the face on the off chance I would slip a punch in, so he used to laugh and tell me I was too good and just wrestle with me. I think his back used to bother him a lot too and kneeling and boxing didn't help.

We had that linoleum that we used for breakdancing and the Whale's Stomach. That also doubled as the floor of our boxing ring. Our basement was a huge hangout for neighborhood kids when my parents weren't home, and even when they were.

They would just let us in that basement and close the door at the top of the stairs sealing us off from sight and sound to them and go about their business if they were home. Or if they weren't it was our little island to rule and do what we pleased.

We would have half days every Wednesday at our Catholic school and it eventually became a known thing that my parents were at work, and we would hold fights. Before long it grew in popularity and everyone used to come over, friends and not friends. Some kids just looking to fight.

With the linoleum as the ring floor, we put a chair at each corner with a string from chair to chair. We would take tuns, with the headgear and gloves and beat the shit out of each other until one kid couldn't take it anymore. There were no rounds, no time limits, just kid vs kid wailing on each other.

Bloody noses sent blood splattering around the room and kids with braces had lips that looked like chopped meat. Eventually kids started bringing their own mouth pieces to protect their lips and teeth from biting through them.

That's why I call it underground boxing in retrospect, not because it was some nefarious underground ring. It did however happen literally underground in our basement, but more importantly it happened without anyone's parents knowing. Kids would come home with black eyes and busted lips and pretend nothing happened.

Kids cheered and screamed and during the days leading up to it at school the fights would be set up in advance. So and so is fighting so and so, Chris is fighting Shinji, Kenny is fighting Andrew, etc.

It wasn't quite a fight club, but it certainly was similar. No rules other than if you fell out of the ring and didn't want to get back in, we would stop the fight. Occasionally an angry kid would chase someone out of the ring and keep swinging but we would break that up.

About a year later my dad took me to the Police Athletic League near the 109th precinct to do PAL Boxing. I lasted about 2 workouts and a sparring match before I realized fighting Catholic school kids in uniforms in our basement was a lot easier than fighting city kids that wanted to be fighters.

My dad was not disappointed, he was just happy that I was able to finally be a kid.

CHAPTER 3

A Ramp Grows in Brooklyn

On a hot, sticky morning in the summer of 1984 or so, our core group met up on Bell Blvd. near the bus stop. We met in front of what would become the one-hour photo, about a block up from Bayside Movie theater at 39th Avenue, as we often did when school was out.

If you grew up in the northeast, and probably other areas as well that got hot and sticky in the summer, a summer morning at 8am meant a cacophony of cicada's making noise in unison. They did it so loudly that it sounded like outer space had a radio playing stuck in between stations.

A cicada, for those that do not know, is a locust looking insect that made a whining noise in unison with a million of other cicadas every morning as the heat kicked in, amplifying the volume to an annoying, although be it not quite deafening backdrop to whatever you were doing.

We were all between 13-15 years old at this point and our parents all at work, so we were home alone, as usual. Also as usual, we would never stay home. On this day it was me, Jimmy Tame, Gibson, and our good friend Trent. All of us wrote graffiti locally this year, with some ventures outside of our neighborhood, but mostly this year and summer was all about skating for us.

We fully embraced the skate and surf culture that was radiating out of California, thanks to icons like Powell and Peralta, and through the pages of Skates on Haight catalogues, Transworld, and Thrasher Magazines. Our wardrobes were filled with surf and skate apparel, sourced directly from mail-order at Skates on Haight and others, snagging deals that local stores couldn't touch. Skate shops became our haunts, not just locally but also in places like Long Beach, where Jimmy was now living with his family. On weekends or during summer breaks, we'd catch the 7 and RR trains, making our way to Manhattan's village to chill at Dream Wheels, Rat Cage, and similar spots.

Back then, the owner of Rat Cage was known for cross-dressing, or being a transvestite, a term used long before it became a topic of broader conversation or controversy. Being from NYC, we were exposed to all walks of life, and nothing fazed us. If someone was cool with us, that's all that mattered. We'd spend a lot of time at the shop, often hanging around well after we were done browsing. Interestingly, Rat Cage was also dabbling in music, producing some of the early hardcore tracks for the Beastie Boys, way before they hit the big time – something we weren't even aware of yet. From what I remember the store was dark inside and was two levels. It's been so long but the allure of that store was above the rest for us when we first started trekking to the village.

Later, there would be another store on 6th avenue called Soho Skates that we would often frequent as well. Each time as part of the journey to and from the Brooklyn Bridge Banks, an iconic skate spot in lower Manhattan. Oddly enough we used to hang out with an older and legendary graffiti writer Kid Panama, of Subway Art fame, he was often at the banks. He had a skateboard with extra trucks on it, called it a 6 skate or 8 skate or something. He wasn't painting much at that time unfortunately for us, or maybe he just didn't want to bring us painting.

In our wanderings, we'd catch wind of urban legends, one of which was a mythical half-pipe in Brooklyn. Rumor had it, this massive ramp was constructed for a professional skateboarding event in Red Hook, Brooklyn, about a year prior, and then abandoned in place and left to decay.

This behemoth of a ramp lay forgotten in a desolate lot, a stone's throw from the local housing projects, and had seen better days, deteriorating under the relentless weather. The scene was completed by a couple of abandoned, charred cars nearby. The local kids weren't into skating, and it seemed neither a welcoming nor safe spot for visitors.

But, fueled by our innate curiosity and thirst for adventure, we were determined to uncover this hidden gem.

Trying to find out more we were going skate shop to skate shop in Lower Manhattan asking questions as if we were detectives on a hot lead. Most people shrugged us off and probably had no idea what we were talking about until one skater overheard us at Dream Wheels. He wrote the street intersection on a piece of torn paper. He gave us no other information, but like a spy he handed us the paper and said something cryptic like, "Go here and find what you're looking for."

"Do you have it?" Gibson asked on that hot sticky morning when he arrived at the meet up.

"Right here." I replied pulling out the little piece of paper with two cross streets written on it, and another piece of paper with the name of a city and a subway station. The town was "Red Hook", the subway station was "Smith and 9th Street", in Brooklyn which might as well been a million miles from where we were standing.

It was going to be a 2-hour journey almost for us. All to seek out a white elephant. With skateboards in hand, we embarked on our journey down to the aforementioned legendary half-pipe skateboard ramp that supposedly sat in a vacant, abandoned lot not far from the Red Hook housing projects in Brooklyn.

We had just enough money on each of us for a bus fare to Main Street to catch the subway and back, and for a subway fare or two just in case we couldn't sneak into the system, and probably an extra $1.25 each. Which at that time in 1984 was enough for a slice and a coke, our typical lunch. All in all, we had about $4 or $5 each that we got from our parents for this quest.

"Have fun," my mom said before she left me the money on that early summer morning in June and then left for work. Fun as if we were going to a local movie. My mom passed away in 2022 and she still never grasped the reality of how far into the dark city we made it back then.

We rode the bus to Main Street Flushing where we descended into the 7-line subway station on Roosevelt Ave. Here we did not have to pay the fare. Sure, we were supposed to, but we just pulled the black gate open, currently unlocked because summer school was just starting. Although we didn't have transit passes anymore, our obvious school kid age gave us all the cover we needed during the still busy morning hour, no one said anything.

We got onto the train and checked the map, which is what you always did, an oddly New York thing and an obvious necessity in the pre tech era. You never knew which trains went to exactly where you were going and although someone already told us the G line stop Smith and 9th, we had no idea which was the best place to transfer to the G coming from where we were, and this was true for even most adults.

The NYC transit system is fairly complex and there are often shorter intermediary routes you can choose to make a trip more direct than just riding to obvious change points like Times Square or Grand Central, etc.

As the train pulls out of the station, we studied the map on the wall. The train then rocks through the short tunnel before ascending to the elevated tracks; we select our station change, probably 74th and Broadway for the F or G, but I don't remember exactly anymore. Also, not a key detail anymore from where I'm sitting.

Riding out of Main Street on the train was always very exciting, even though I was already doing it regularly for Bronx Science, it wasn't often with my friends in the later morning. The train is less crowded after 9am, and it usually wasn't a bright sunny summer day like this one. The 7 train rides through Flushing into Corona and passes the US Open on the left and Shea Stadium on the right. Not long after is Flushing Meadow Park with many of the iconic New York sights in view, including the Manhattan skyline ahead to the west.

We changed trains and rode the G or F into the elevated Smith and 9th street station which was very elevated from what I remember. Oddly enough I would never ride the train getting on and off at this station again after this day. Not really because of any sort of trauma, but just never had any reason to return.

Once in the Smith and 9th station we exited the train, stopping again at the large map by the token booth downstairs. Looking for the cross streets, we got our bearings and then went to the token booth to ask for some additional help finding the intersection. Token booth clerks were usually pretty helpful at this time and told us it was about 15 blocks or so away and pointed us in the right direction.

We skated through the neighborhood, on sidewalks, and streets, "Shredding" as they called it, I mean, we weren't all that impressive as skaters, but we could rip through a neighborhood slapping tails and making a racket like most.

And then we saw it!

In an empty lot stood an enormous half pipe, 10 foot high at each side and about 16 feet wide. There was one full foot of "vert" at the top of the transitions making it very difficult for novices to skate. It was the largest ramp we had ever seen at this point in our lives. And true to the rumors, we could now see it was weathering significantly.

The lack of use meant no upkeep. The neighborhood had other problems that didn't include removing what was trash to the community either. So, this ramp just stood, surrounded by weeds growing up through the cracks in an old unused previously paved lot.

The plywood was brown and splintering a bit from a few years in the weather. It indeed looked like it was probably built by Thrasher or some other sponsored skate event that took place the previous years.

It did not have anyone skating on it, and my sense now looking back was that it wasn't a neighborhood that was big into skating the in the mid 1980s. And now I realize it was mostly abandoned for a reason. I'm sure some older skaters may have frequented it by driving up in cars, skating and leaving, but I doubt many took the train from as far as we did.

We climbed to the top platform on one of the sides and thought about dropping in. We had no pads, the one foot of vertical plus the nine-foot-tall transition was terrifying looking down.

"No fucking way," I said. "Not doing it."

We all looked at each other for a moment before Gibson started skating slowly back and forth trying to build up speed starting at the bottom. Trent and I watched from the top.

"Watch out!" Exclaimed Trent to our surprise. He was going to go for it.

Trent stepped up; he lapped the tail of his skateboard onto the top coping with the board extending off the sheer drop. Rear foot holding the board in place he quipped something under his breath. "Here goes nothin."

Putting his front foot now onto the extended skateboard, leaning forward, in he went. A common error skaters make when learning to drop in on new ramps or bigger ramps is they do not lean forward enough, they ride in on the back wheels only and can never catch up with the momentum and by the time the reach the bottom the board shoots out from under them sending them backward in a dangerous and awkward fall which can hurt their wrists or backs, or heads. And it also propels the board forward at a high rate of speed where the board sometimes shoots off the side of the ramp into the air, a dangerous projectile now.

We knew a kid that got hit in the mouth from such a runaway board and he lost three of his front teeth in the incident.

But Trent was an experienced skater, he knew the deal with leaning forward, so he totally committed. But what he had never felt before was one full foot of vertical surface that top of the ramp before the transition, or curved part, would start. Him leaning far enough forward for our previous ramps was too far by just a smidge on this completely vertical surface now. He floated a little too long and got out ahead of the board, the opposite problem. He basically just fell ten feet straight down to the bottom in a slam that sounded as painful as it looked, earning him a sore shoulder and some splinters.

Being kids we all laughed as he dusted himself off, wiped up a few minor scrapes and cuts with his t-shirt. Eventually we all started skating the ramp from within, using motion to gradually get higher and higher and do kick turns, and even small airs at the coping, and having a blast for about the next hour.

As I mentioned the ramp was mostly vacant and I'm sure it was rarely skated, our activity now drew the attention of some neighborhood kids who started watching us. Mostly black kids watching 3 white kids and one black kid skate a ramp where they lived. As time went on the kids seemed to multiply more and more. Something we were very cognizant of.

Before too much longer it became palpable, uncomfortable. I mean we were already doing graffiti, and riding trains and hanging out in neighborhoods that could lead to trouble, so we knew what was starting to happen.

Some of the younger kids started to ask us questions, that eventually led to them trying to figure out where we were from, it was at this point we knew we should get the fuck out of there. But we also knew we had to do it smartly because we can't just turn and run. They are right here and right on top of us and likely would catch some of us if not all.

We no sooner said to them that we were going to run down the block to the store to get drinks that one of the younger ones says to us, "This ramp ain't free, you have to pay to ride it".

To which Gibson responded, "We don't have any money."

"What about the money for the drinks?" quipped back another one.

Now, we were a long way from home, but we also weren't the type of kids that were going to let other kids go through our pockets either.

In the heat of the building tension, Gibson jumped on his board and started skating away yelling to them, "I'll be right back just getting those drinks." We all followed Gibson and did the same as three of the younger kids that were closest, started jogging after us, following us.

The rest of them stayed behind giving me a momentary feeling of relief because I thought to myself, we could kick these three younger kids' asses if we had to.

We approached the store up ahead which was about midway between the ramp and the station, we were very thirsty by now. Plus, as I mentioned there was only three younger kids following us, what were they going to do?

We went inside to get "quarter waters" which is a story in themselves. If you grew up in the city at this time you know what those were. These little 6oz plastic bottle with a foil cap that contained a flavored water liquid in orange or grape or maybe punch too. They cost 25 cents, and we drank these all of the time. The rapper 50 Cent years later would reference these in one of his albums.

The three kids made it to the store, and as we walked out one of them said "What's up with Supreme's money?"

"Who is Supreme?" I replied.

"The guy you got to pay to skate that ramp" said one of the kids.

"We already told you we don't got no more money, only enough for these quarter waters," Gibson said, again, getting on his board and us following as we skated to the station.

When we got to the station however, there they all were, about 15 of them, older kids included!

Holy shit! Stopping at the store was a stupid mistake, what we didn't realize is they knew if we came by train there would be no way else for us to leave so they went to the station to find us, sure enough we skated up just as they got there. In a moment of panic, we ran up all of the steps, which seemed to go on forever, with these 15 kids running up behind us.

We got to the turnstiles and like in the movie "The Warriors" we jumped right over, then so did these 15 kids chasing us, up the stairs again onto the Queens bound side.

There was a lot of yelling between us and this group of kids. Two MTA workers were emptying the trash, along with about ten other people waiting for the train. The group of 15 kids has now surrounded us on the platform.

"We already told you we don't got no money!" Gibson screamed at them.

"Supreme said to ask y'all what's up with them boards then!" they screamed back at him, meaning they would take the skateboards.

I looked toward one of the transit workers for help and he said exactly this – "You all got them boards; you better use them!" which immediately set off a melee.

But something weird was happening in this melee, the 15 kids were all black, and Gibson is black, and they primarily were interested in Gibson, they didn't seem to focus on us three at all.

Maybe it was because Gibson was a year older than us, and by far the strongest looking, or maybe because he was the one that seemed to be doing most of the talking. But when they set it off, it was Gibson they all started swinging on, putting us in a position where we were behind them pulling them off of Gibson until Gibson rose up like Hercules with the skateboard, bloodied nose, and torn shirt he whacked a couple of them with the board and was chasing another one when they started to back off.

At this point we were also pushing them back and I think Gibson's reaction with violence to meet their violence caught them off guard. Plus, like I said he was very strong, and I'm sure whoever got hit with his board felt that for real.

It turned mostly into a screaming match now as the train pulled in and we got on, alone. The other 15 kids did not, and we left the station on the train bound for Queens.

"FUCKKKKK!" shouted Gibson in anger as the train left the station, we all surrounded him trying to find out if he was ok, also excited at our, his, somewhat of a triumph in what could have been a very bad situation. As the train rocked down the tracks, us cheering on Gibson still, eventually he relished in the moment, his moment, as all kids do after you fight your fight. We were going to live to tell this tale, again, it was part of life, part of our life.

But still there was a sadness with us. As we finally settled across the back row seat on the Q13 city bus for the final leg of our journey back to Bayside, we sat in silence. We had still not eaten lunch, hungry, exhausted. We felt somehow attacked by our city, betrayed in a sense. Something that has happened before and something that would happen again.

The bus finally turned onto Bell Blvd. and that feeling of being home was complete. We got off the bus where we got on and saw our good friend Alex Rowens' bike upside down in front of "Creamy Egg Cream," a magazine store with arcade games in the back.

The upside-down bike was something we commonly did back then, you would take your BMX bike and invert it parked resting on the seat and handlebars. The reasoning was we never had kickstands anymore so it was a stable way to set the bike, but more importantly it would take a would-be thief longer to grab the bike and flip it over to ride away.

The sadness quickly dispelled, euphoria taking its place, we felt like we had just won a prize, and in a way we did. We had a victory on the mean streets of New York City in the 1980s. We rushed the store and surrounded Alex. Screaming in his face telling him the story of what just happened. We spilled out onto the street all jumping and celebrating. I mean the story was exciting, but the underlying event was scary and dark, to which Alex replied, "Fuck! I wish I was there!"

And his response sums up perfectly what life was all about for us. There was no social media, almost no TV, no means for any experiences beyond what you lived through. And when you heard your friends went out on any given day and "Saw a dead body," you wished you had seen it too.

No matter how grotesque, no matter how scary.

CHAPTER 4

SCRAP WOOD

Our hunt for the perfect skate spot was unyielding. Inspired by the endless skate spots, pools, and ramps we'd see in videos from California, we found ourselves craving the same in the concrete jungle of New York City—a challenging quest, to say the least. However, fortune smiled upon us when we stumbled upon a pool within a newly constructed school that sat above the Cross Island Parkway looking across the bay at Great Neck. I still have no idea what school this is to this day, might have been a hospital type of school or some other medical related school facility. It had that look, made of orangish split face brick with sandstone accents.

This place remained under construction and unfilled for more than three years before its doors finally opened, delays in construction were common in the 1980s. One peek through the window revealed our makeshift skate haven in the form of an empty newly constructed indoor pool. Without hesitation, we broke in, spending countless days reveling in our secret spot, skating the empty pool, and embracing our youthful recklessness. Yet, an empty pool wasn't the ramp we dreamed of. The main problem with it was it was shallow, about 4 or 5 feet at the deepest which made the transitions steep. It was possible to get up to grind quickly and acrobatically, but we were never going to be able to do airs or handplants on the coping.

We'd set off on expeditions to uncover a secluded ramp in Hicksville, it was a cool ramp, also large, in the middle of a wooded area, but not very convenient. We needed one of our parents to drive us, then come back to get us, which they never wanted to do nor were they even around to do it.

We'd visited another one out towards South Long Island, a private ramp owned by the hardcore band THE CRUMBSUCKERS. But venturing there was also something we could only do when our parents were willing to play chauffeur. What we needed was our own ramp.

The largest ramp we built and one of our first was a complete halfpipe in my back yard, with no permission from my parents. My dad just came home from work one day and saw this monolithic structure of framework taking up most of the yard, and he didn't say anything, I mean what could he say. Looking back now, having my own kid, there must have been a solace in knowing your kid was safe at home in this city in those days. I even feel that now.

But before he even saw that he started to see a small lumber yard being assembled on the back patio, little by little over about a month, neatly stacked 2x4 piles, plywood, nails, and other supplies. He never asked where it came from, but by the time we were ready to build it literally looked like a lumber yard.

We creatively acquired the wood from the surrounding area, liberating it from construction sites and houses under renovation. Nearby, they were also constructing that school close to the Cross Island, the one with the empty pool, offering views of the bay, all conveniently located within roughly a half-mile radius of my home.

It started off with us approaching some of these sites during the day. Me, Gibson, Jimmy, Cheeky, Tim, Trent, and asking if they had any "Scrap wood". As Gibson would call it. And he had this way of speaking sometimes, mostly on purpose, emphatically and comically like the way Chris Rock speaks today, and he would ask the workers, "You guys got any 'scrap wood'?" Which usually was met with a no, and he would push harder, emphasizing the "Scrap wood" vernacular in a comical way, "Scrap wood? I need some scrap wooood!" As the workers were usually shushing us away by now.

It was apparent that it was going to be very rare that anyone was going to contribute any wood to our cause willingly.

Which is when we decided, as already lawless young teens, that we were just going to go back to these places at night and help ourselves. Looking back now, quite a daunting task, because we needed about 16 sheets of 4x8 plywood for the ramp, and about 100 2x4s, and if you've ever loaded those things into your vehicle from the cart you know it's work. Now imagine not having a vehicle, and 6 of us carrying three sheets of plywood, 2 kids on each, walking through the street at night for 25 minutes or so, quite a sight and quite a lot of work.

But we did it, night after night, slowly siphoning off supplies from these worksites, and slowly building our own collection of supplies. Before long we realized we could use our skateboards as dollies, wagons, sometimes we'd even take the wheelbarrows from the jobsite and abandon them in the park across from my house.

We stole nails, tools, whatever we could get our hands on and over the course of a few weeks we finally had everything we needed.

But before we made our last run for the final sheets of plywood there was one funny night when we were on Bell Blvd. We were hanging out waiting for the sun to set so we could go get the wood.

There was a metal guardrail at the Citibank parking lot, and we were doing skateboard tricks, ollie-ing up and tail slapping to grinding the guardrail, when Gibson slipped his skateboard over the rail which had a sharp back edge, skinning his shin pretty badly. Cheeky who was quite abrasive, but a very good friend of Gibson's used to make racial slurs at him from time to time, something that was done in jest as they would both go at it pretty good, Cheeky having a family with some dwarfism and Gibson would get on him about "Them midgets" too. All in good fun most of the time, but sometimes they would get under each other's skin.

And this was one of those times. When Gibson skinned his leg, Cheeky responded, "haha look at the Ni##a skinned his leg!" And started really ribbing him while Gibson was on the ground in pain, and from the ground Gibson responded back, "haha well this Ni##a ain't gonna help you go steal no woooood!" Which immediately made Cheeky serious, "Shut the fuck up dick, you better help us." As finishing this ramp was a priority of ours at this time.

It was a hysterical exchange which ended as they usually did, everyone friends, and yes, we did go steal wood that night.

The conversation on the approach to the site that night was funny too. We needed more help and Cheeky had been advocating we bring Dave Vamer on the next run because Vamer was big and strong even though a year younger than us. And as we were approaching the site, there was someone there and we stepped back into the shadows worried he might have seen us but more so we worried that he might be there because he noticed wood was going missing and he was investigating or keeping an eye on the place.

From the shadows Cheeky said to us, "I wish Vamer was here right now" and when we asked why, Cheeky said "Vamer will slap a man right in his face." To which we all laughed, quietly of course, while we waited in the shadows for the guy to get in his truck and leave, which he eventually did. And we proceeded to go into the site and take stacks of wood, two children on each stack, carrying it through the night, with our skateboard dollies, as we made our way down the street.

Gibson was the one with the experience on the tools, particularly the circular saw, I mean we did some hammering and caught on pretty quickly with driving nails, but the circular saw was a bit scary, it was loud, and we were very cautious of the notion of it cutting our fingers off. So, Gibson did all of the sawing, we would hold the wood in place for him, help him mark it off, but he would almost exclusively operate the saw. We would of course use hand saws on 2x4s but the circular saw on the plywood was all Gibson. At least on the first ramp we built.

We managed to frame it rather quickly. First, we cut out the transitions for the sides using a string and a pencil to create the radius. Next, we framed the 2x4s across each end of the half-pipe, and then we framed the flat on the floor before connecting everything. This entire cutting process took about one day, and by the next day, we had erected the frame. This was the sight that greeted my dad when he came home. As a father now, I can only imagine what he must have thought. Back then, he had no idea what a half-pipe was, and to him, the framed structure probably looked like we were building a house in the backyard. And as far as he knew, we had never even used a tool before.

But as I mention, me and my brother were computer hackers, my brother had appeared on a news story the year before for kids and coding computers, my dad knew we were high IQ. And like little AIs, he knew we learned things on our own very quickly, so nothing phased him anymore. He just shrugged it off and did his thing before returning to work after a few hours of sleep.

The ramp was completed in a couple of days, and it was a bit late the day we finished; we worked through dinner. Our back yard shared fence lines with 5 other houses, and the properties in Bayside Queens for the most part were not all that big, so the houses were not far beyond the fence lines.

We didn't even think to fill in the empty spaces beneath the ramp with insulation or anything to dampen sound, it was like a huge wooden drum at both ends. About to be beaten on by 100-pound kids on wheels. There were probably ten of us gathered in my yard at this point, it was a coronation of sorts, we were about to christen this ramp and send it off on its journey.

Trent was always going to go first, he climbed up to the top of the platform, 8 feet high, which was high for a ramp built by 12-year-olds. We also included one foot of complete vertical at the top of each side, something we later found out was a mistake making it extremely tough to skate. It added a huge degree of difficulty to our learning curve and made our first "drop ins" quite daunting. A few months later we would modify the ramp, cutting off the vert and shortening the overall height in the process. But not yet. It was all or nothing for us here.

Trent placed his board on the lip as he did in Brooklyn and many times before. The lip here made of split PVC pipe coping, typical on ramps back then. He leaned in and VROOOM! And BOOOM, and VROOOM and BOOM! He went back and forth from side to side, to the cheers of us all, but my god was that ramp loud and it hadn't even dawned on us yet that it was getting close to 10pm, we were oblivious, and all took turns shredding this thing (the best we could, as the vert limited us even getting back up to the coping for the most part. The noise had to be monstrous and repetitive and never ending for my neighbors.

One of my neighbors came out into his back yard and yelled in the night at us, "hey it's getting late, why don't you guys check in for the night." A perfectly reasonable request. The voice seemed to come from nowhere and everywhere, we weren't even sure which direction. The "Check in" phrasing might have been a little awkward too and my brother picked right up on it and yelled back, "Check in where? A hotel?"

I mean imagine being a grown man yelling to a bunch of kids at 11pm on a weeknight to wrap up the "Party" of sorts and call it a night and you get a response back from a squeaky 12-year-old like that?

"Don't be a wise ass! You know what I mean, it's getting late." Responded the random voice from the dark.

The conversation devolved from there, and it wasn't a pleasant exchange and eventually in the next half hour we wrapped it up, but it was a grudge my brother would carry for a little while. Who was that guy? He speculated and tried to guess which house was his. He eventually made up his mind that it was the house on a diagonal from our yard, that shares only a corner lot line, not the house directly behind us, and not the house on either side of us, but diagonally back from the right.

Our house has several gables in the roof and where they connected to the flat garage roof there was like an area hidden from the world, you could walk up the slope and see over and out into the street and the neighbors' properties, but once you went down into the roof valley no one could see you. And this was a favorite spot of ours, and my brother's, where we and he would shoot CO_2 BB Guns breaking out car windows driving by, usually speeding.

It was a sense of vigilante justice for my brother because a year or so earlier my mother had this vintage OPAL car parked in front of our house and someone speeding around the corner totaled it in a hit and run. My brother at that point took out his revenge on cars he thought were speeding. I mean imagine the balls to shoot out windows on cars in front of your own house.

From up there we could also see, as I just mentioned, into our neighbors' yards and see the house of the guy we suspected was yelling at us that night.

While we were skating the ramp another night my brother was up in his roof spot looking around and he could see a guy in the house looking out his window which was brightly lit, the guy was looking towards our house, because of the noise again.
My brother started shooting him with the BB GUN breaking his windows, and the guy hit the deck, then came back up to peak and my brother shot him up several times.

The guy ran out of the room and out the front door and my brother hurried into the house soon followed by a POUNDING on my dad's front door.

My dad answered and this guy was there with bloody welts on him screaming about what happened. He tried to push his way in, but my dad pushed him back out of the house and told him he would pay for the windows and to get the "Fuck off " our property.

My dad was a fairly quiet guy publicly but like I said, he was a wartime Marine and would take no shit from anyone, especially when it came to his kids.

My dad was furious though and tossed my brother a whooping that night and paid for the guy's windows and we never heard from that guy again.

My dad and my brother would go at it pretty good. But never me, my dad would never raise a hand to me because I spent 8 years in that children's hospital. My illness took such a toll on my dad that once I got healthy, he treated me like I was made of glass.

My mom on the other hand had no such sympathy for me, it seemed her job was to make up for the lack of discipline towards me by my father and it was my job to keep her busy. And I was good at my job, and she was good at hers.

Getting whooped with the buckle end of the belt became a favorite pastime of mine.

CHAPTER 5

A Brooklyn Love Story, that never was.

My childhood development as I said earlier was retarded, and before you get up in arms thinking I continue using words that are not acceptable, I'm not. My childhood development was retarded after being diagnosed with Leukemia and spending much of my time in a children's hospital. And although the word retarded may have fallen completely out of favor today, that was the word used by doctors and therapists to describe my late physical development and social development because of my condition. Hence, I still use that word today in speaking of my medical history.

While normal kids were learning to socialize in groups and learn about girls and boys and other things that become apparent to children in school, I was in a children's hospital reading books.

By the 4th grade I started to be integrated more and more into the activities of my elementary school as I has survived some of the most dangerous parts of my disease that made it impossible for me to play with other kids in the years prior. The disease would incidentally go on to haunt me for the rest of my life with several terminal dates, all of which I have survived, and currently I sit in yet another terminal window with end stage disease possibilities within a year or two.

One thing I have learned, besides the power of the reflection brought on by facing your own mortality is, no one on either parent's side of my family will ever die. I mean my mom's mom and dad were both dead by their thirties, but one died in a coal mine and the other battled addiction in the wake of losing her partner. And on my dad's side they just keep living. Including both of my parents who never even saw a doctor until they were in their 80s, like not even for checkups.

These crazy genetics have been underestimated by my doctors time and time again when putting an expiration date on myself, so now I pretty much just shrug it off. I had a dangerous surgery last year, looked like the end was very near, but I've since rebuilt myself again in the gym and feel great, and yes, I am going to die, eventually. We all are.

I should probably add, that since my original writing of this chapter, both my mom and dad have passed on. My mom at 83, a bit early but a victim of her own somewhat unhealthy lifestyle. Eventually brought to her demise by the negligence of a nursing facility and a terrible sepsis infection. My dad less than a year later at 94, mostly died of lack of will to live after losing his wife, my mother. Had circumstances been different for both of them, I am certain they would both still be living.

I am already in my 50's, and at some point, when I die, they will declare my disease killed me but did it really?

I have been outrunning this grim reaper since I was a baby, and he still hasn't caught me. By the time I die it will be official, I lived a complete life, a complete lifespan. Even if I die in my mid 50s, that sucks, but that still was a lifespan, what did I miss? My sixties and seventies? You can have them since I never wanted them anyway. Easy to say now, and I used to say that about my thirties and forties when I was a teenager. Once I am sixty years old, I am certain I will want my sixties and seventies and anything else this universe sees fit to allow me.

I digress, my development was slowed as a child but by the 4th grade I was now in school most of the time with my "peers" trying to socialize having started learning to socialize just now at 9-years-old, with no experience. I would still be taken out of school every week and back to the hospital for treatments and infusions but for the most part I was going to have a childhood. In theory anyway.

One of the first things I did when socializing with healthy girls was fall madly in love with a girl in my glass named Michelle, but she had no clue. I didn't even know what it meant to like a girl, but I knew I liked her. And one day I was being picked up from school at 11am again to be returned to the hospital for a treatment, sickly looking and pale, and one of the boys in the class quipped to another boy, "He's so lucky, he always gets to leave school early."

Michelle overheard this and being a nice girl, she turned to them in anger and quipped back, "He's not lucky, he's dying!" to shut them up. And her saying that hurt more than any biopsy ever would. Michelle, whom I had hoped with all my heart would someday see me as a child she might have a future friendship with just coldly declared that I had no future.

Man, that hurt. I don't hold it against her in my eyes looking back, she was a child too. None of us had a clue about life yet. Only difference was I already knew life could end at any time, most kids don't think like that or really ponder what that means. Growing up in the oncology wing of a children's hospital you catch on quick. Many of your peers pass on from month to month, replaced by new versions of the walking dead. Kids facing an end that isn't even considered by most for another 60 years or more.

Suddenly at 10 years old things were looking up for me, I did have almost 70 blood transfusions in New York City between 1975 and 1980 right at the epicenter of the start of the AIDS epidemic, but other than that I was good to go. A surgery to remove some of the disease was successful and I remissed almost overnight.

Going forward, health insurance requirements until college would require me get monthly HIV tests which were always fun. Nothing like being told every month there is no chance you haven't contracted another fatal disease on top of your already fatal disease.

Statistically I was a goner, but genetically it would turn out I was almost immune.

My mom was possibly Jewish, we didn't even realize that until she passed, my wife going through her things found evidence of such. There was family evidence of Jewish heritage, we knew that, but it never dawned on any of us that she might have been 100% non-practicing Jewish. She married into a Catholic family.

Genetic testing would reveal she was partially Ashkenazi Jewish, at least one of her grandparents. And it turns out Ashkenazi Jews have a much higher resistance to HIV which some of my doctors think is the only plausible reason I would not have contracted it.

By the age of 15 I was writing graffiti almost every day, mostly local but I was commuting to Bronx Science daily for High School, my aspirations of writing on trains would come to fruition later that year.

I still, at this point in my life, had only one other interaction with a girl when at 11 years old my 14-year-old babysitter told me how she had never kissed a boy. She wanted to kiss a boy at school but didn't know how. She asked if she could kiss me and I didn't know what to say, so she kissed me. She "made out" with me for almost half an hour one night while my parents were at a dinner with a cousin that needed financial help.

I felt nothing during that experience because I so didn't even understand what a girl was still and I might as well have been kissing a boy or human or dog, it meant nothing.

Now at 16 and still, I never had a meaningful conversation with a girl in High School. I started hanging out in Brooklyn with my, soon to be close friend, Chino BYI, a lot. And he was dating a girl in Astoria at the time named Jasmine. We would occasionally take the train to her house, and she'd come out to Astoria Park with us, and I'd see them fool around as I walked around taking marker tags, still kind of oblivious to the whole girl/guy thing.

A few years earlier in the early 1980's was the NYC Punk Rock scene, which started in the 1970's but for me started in 1982 at 12 years old. We were getting mohawks and colored hair and piercings and some tattoos even before we hit 15 years old.

There were about 5 of us in our core group ranging in ages from 13-15 with me being close to the youngest and one of my 14-year-old friends named Vamer being a kid that was large and looked at least 17 or 18 despite he was still actually a child.

This was the same kid Cheeky referred to as someone that could smack a grown man right in his face, due to his size and advanced maturity for his age.

We toted our skateboards and blasted punk rock tunes, along with hardcore tracks that often clashed with punk's ethos. Yet, at that age, it was all about rebelling against the norm, and we were into it all, including the Dead Kennedys, who rocked a punk vibe but with lyrics that annoyed punk rockers and some hardcore fans alike.

We'd disappear for days on end, and my parents were pretty convinced we were off experimenting with drugs or being gay. But there was little they could do to rein us in. Once I left the house while my parents were at work, I was gone, sometimes prompting my parents to call the police, which was rare for my parents. They would never call the police, but when it came to their children missing, I guess they made an exception. It hardly mattered anyway; they seldom caught up with me to drag me back home.

Just off of Northern Blvd in Flushing Queens, there was an industrial building called "Company Electric," complete with loading docks on the backside of a large, fenced property that sat right up against railroad tracks. The property was large, and we would jump the back fence and skate the loading docks and just hang out there at night.

One day some cars pulled in and it turns out the main gates weren't even locked they were just pulled shut, so these older kids ranging in ages from 17-22 would pull in there at night and leave the music on in one of the cars and drink and do drugs and just hang, also listening to punk rock music and skating.

They saw us one day and were cool so it just became this sort of neighborhood thing, where we would all be, all the time and we all got along great. Albeit odd that older kids were hanging out with kids our age and drinking with us and doing drugs with us. At least two of these kids were or would go on to become famous in the skate scene and music scene, for privacy's sake I will not elaborate on their identities.

Sometimes they would even pile us into their cars and take us places. Two of the older kids were gay, probably the first two gay kids we knew. There were also several older girls ranging in ages from 17-22 also that would often show up in their own car or be packed into the cars with us.

These girls were oddly good looking now that I think about it, much too good looking to be trashy punk rock girls doing drugs and getting fucked behind a loading dock by the tracks. But none the less there they were. Two in particular were Veronica who had huge boobs, and bleached colored hair with bright colors in it, fishnet stockings, dock marten boots, and her friend Marilyn, a brunette in a short new wave partially shaved hair cut with an amazing shape and bright red lips. And Marilyn's "Thing" as it was known was to devirginize little boys that hadn't had sex yet.

Veronica started dating our friend Dave Vamer who looked older than he was, and Marylin was with one of the older dudes too, both of these girls about 18 years old.

Veronica comes over to me one day and asked me, just like this, "Are you a virgin? Have you ever been fucked?" And I was 13 or 14 at the time and terrified but I answered her yes, I was a virgin, sheepishly and skated away. Later she came up to me again with her friend Marylin and they were hitting on me, two 18-year-old girls, hitting on a 13-year-old boy behind a warehouse on the tracks at 2am on a Tuesday night. I was scared but at the same time I was curious.

A couple of nights of this kind of flirting and propositioning found me in the back of one of these older kid's cars, nervous and trembling with Marylin who was kissing me and undoing my pants.

I was so nervous nothing wound up happening, either because she sensed it and felt bad for me or maybe I just wasn't functional physically in that way given my fear and awkwardness.

All this however was in furtherance of the awkwardness my childhood illness caused with delaying my social interactions. I was still yet to be normally interested in a girl that knew I was alive, now approaching 16 years old. Relative to the ages that boys and girls typically start to notice each other, I was a senior citizen by now.

I started hanging out in Brooklyn more and more. At 17 years old my next-door neighbor gave my dad an old Honda Civic I could use, his logic being that he didn't want me asking to drive my dad's Cadillacs and giving me my own car was the way to avoid that. You will learn a bit more about my dad's relationship with my neighbor in an upcoming chapter, in retrospect it made sense what they did.

Using this Honda, I would start driving to pick up my friend Chino more and more. One of the things we would do that summer was go to his girl's house in Astoria and hang out with her and her friends.

One of her friends was a 16-year-old girl named Becky from Park Slope Brooklyn. If you read my first book you might remember her as one of the two girls I went to a club with a few times. My interest in her was that she was cute, smart, and went to a specialized High School like me.

Her interest in me, assuming she actually was interested, was I was smart, went to a specialized high school and was a mix between the street kids she normally hung around with from Brooklyn and a smart perceivably good kid.

She was the first real girl I knew that might have realized I was alive. I tried to play it cool, but I am sure she knew I was awkward with girls and have never really talked to one before in a real friend context.

We used to stay up late in my car or in clubs discussing our futures and the differences in our goals and it used to frustrate her that I didn't care much what became of me 20 years down the line. Compared to others in Bronx Science at the time, I was one of the few that by my senior year wasn't eying an Ivy League institution and pursing that dream with many of my classmates.

I couldn't see the future, I could not see it because my first 9 developmental years I learned, the hard way, that I might not have a future at all. This became ingrained deep within my subconscious to this day and continues to plague me with a sense of impulsiveness leading to bad decision making.

This impetuousness was probably appealing to her looking back and we started to talk constantly and hang out often, mostly with others as I never pursued much of a dating type of situation. I just didn't know how. We'd continue to go to clubs, dark, fantastically hedonistic places where we would take random drugs and forget what planet we were on.

The vibe of clubs was crazy back then, people were doing the hardest drugs right in the open. People would have sex in the clubs, in bathrooms, in dark corners, stairwells etc. It was almost a fever dream some of these nights, like a guy might be walking by half naked with a horse head on top of his own, and the next day you might remember that and wonder if that really happened. And yes, more often than not it really happened.

One night the four of us, Chino and his girl, Me and Becky were hanging out in Astoria Park. We were walking around when Dave and his girl started fooling around on a park bench. The obvious thing to do here would have been to take my girl's hand and walk over to our own secluded park bench and start kissing or something. Except that I still had never kissed a girl in a normal situation.

So instead of seizing the moment to be romantic, I started walking around the park taking marker tags as usual with Becky following me having a casual conversation. She didn't even think anything weird of me at this point, evident by the ride home.

I let Chino drive my car since he was preparing to get his own driver's license. His permit required him to be in the car with an adult driver, but in the catalogue of crimes we committed daily this was in fine print on page one million. No one even gave that part of it a second thought. Even any cops that might have pulled us over.

The girls were in the backseat, and we arrived back at Jasmine's house to drop his girl off first before making our way back to Brooklyn. When we pulled up at Becky's brownstone in Park Slope, I leaned the seat forward to let her out, not even getting out of the car. My own behavior now embarrasses me in retrospect.

Becky leaned back in and started kissing me on the lips so suddenly that I was stuck in a gaze forward and not reciprocating at all. After a second, she stopped and awkwardly said good night obviously confused by my lack of what she perceived was interest in her, or girls in general, I think.

As we drove off, Chino went on to tell me how hot she and shared a story about another friend of his that had dated her prior. I took this story to mean the opposite of what he was telling it to me for. He was obviously encouraging the relationship and as guys go, giving me a "big up" for having her be into me.

But I immediately thought – damn, she is with another dude and not interested in me. I was so confused.
Our so-called relationship would last another few months with a physical relationship still not developing due to my own obtuseness. We went to the usual clubs and hung out with the group of friends in common often. She went on to personify Brooklyn with her being attached to my Brooklyn friends and our entire group which was largely from Brooklyn.

Her brother oddly enough would fist fight another friend of mine from Bayside in an unrelated incident around the same time. I developed a graffiti war with Chino and his friends in Brooklyn. One I stupidly started by going over his tag outside his girl's house.

I was reacting to his relationship with a small-time graffiti writer from Bayside that gained popularity by sidling up to known graffiti writers. I'm not going to get too much into this here nor do I really hold a grudge but at the time he was annoying to me.

This kid went over me in front of Chino's girl's house when he was with Chino and Chino took a tag with him. In my mind I assumed because Chino was with this Bayside writer that he cosigned his going over me which infuriated me the night I saw it.

I was out with Chino's girlfriend and my pseudo girlfriend Becky when we were dropping Jasmine off. We all saw that they went over my tag, and it was embarrassing to me.

Soon after I dropped Becky off in Park Slope, I went past the building Chino lived in which wasn't far from there and I went over his throw up on his own building alley. Something I never should have done.

Then I went back by his girl's house and went over them there. They all started going over me and it became known that I was no longer welcome in Brooklyn, amongst other things. Before too long I apologized to Chino, and we are cool to this day with him being one of my close friends.

Becky took a bit of an attitude with me when they told her I was no longer welcome which kind of made me mad too, but more so confused than mad. Our relationship was already a disaster in a traditional sense because I was incapable of having a relationship in the first place.

I went by her house late one rainy night on my way home from the city. There was a power outage from what I can remember. She let me in, and we went up to her room and hung out in candlelight with the rain pouring outside. I was soaked because I had been out doing throw ups in the rain by myself and she helped take off my wet clothes and a gave me a dry t-shirt of her brothers to put on.

We sat on her bed in the dark, I lay there looking at the flickering candlelight on the ceiling. Having read and loved Edgar Allen Poe's entire catalogue by now, I was always mesmerized by candlelight shadows. I often allowed myself to fall deeply hypnotized while drifting off into a dream. I am not sure what I was thinking of at this moment anymore when it was interrupted by her rolling into me and putting her arm across me. Still, I did not break my stare at the ceiling. Unaware of reality.

After a minute or two she interrupted my semi-consciousness, "Chris!" she said to get my attention. I rolled my head towards her, our faces just one inch apart as I looked at her. If I did it all over again, we would have kissed at that moment. But in that moment, I was paralyzed.

She was 17 years old by now, still a child as was I. She was confused and I guess I deserved what she said.

"You are such a weirdo." Before she rolled over and went to sleep. I would leave about 20 minutes later, not even saying goodbye and that was the last time I would see or speak to her.

In 2016, twenty-eight years had passed since that night and since I had spoken to her or saw her. I was working as an executive at a publicly traded fashion company and was at our corporate offices in Greensboro, North Carolina at my favorite hotel in that city where I stay often.

There was a leadership conference event in the hotel at this time I was there, and I was on the packed elevator coming down to the restaurant one night for dinner. The elevator stopped at a few other floors, with me standing in the back. People would get on at each stop, making the elevator more and more crowded. Pushing me all the way to the back wall.

On the last stop a girl got on and did a double take, on her second look she looked like she saw a ghost, and she did.

"Hello Rebecca... Yeah it's me." I said with a tone so common as if I saw her every day.

She got off at the bottom and waited for me, perplexed.

We met for drinks later that night and caught up. Eventually getting it all out there. Obviously, I fucked all of that up back when we were kids.

We stay in touch now after that serendipity in Greensboro. She has her own family as do I. Not sure what she wonders about me but obviously my life is full of wondering.

In a more recent conversation with her via text she revealed that if she had known I was sick as a child and had some issues she would have been much more aggressive. She took my lack of forwardness as disinterest. And as most girls, they like to be pursued by boys that want them.

It's hard sometimes looking back, and this was a difficult coming of age situation for both of us. Humans have an innate vulnerability that often makes life a lot harder than it needs to be. Humans play games with each other, they hold back true feelings, not even because they want to play games, more so I think because we are so afraid to be hurt, to be rejected.

Graffiti was also a weird and difficult outlet back then. Today, motivations for kids doing graffiti are often social. Back then it was the opposite. Many graffiti writers were driven to graffiti by loneliness. Many nights graffiti writers would feel outcast by the world around them and disappear into train tunnels alone or with other similar feeling peers.

It was easier for me to just go do throw-ups by myself than it was to talk about my feelings with a girl I liked. We had no phones back then, no text. There was not a constant communication. If you were thinking of someone while you were out, you might try to call them from a payphone. But if they didn't answer or weren't home, it might hurt, and it often did. That part might not have changed much. The hurt.

But graffiti had a way of putting the hurt behind you, the streets loved you, the streets didn't judge. In fact, if you went and painted a nice top to bottom, the night felt like you accomplished something. Your peers might commend you for it the next time they see you. You would become a juggernaut again. You didn't need girls, or boys, you were going to do what you do regardless.

CHAPTER 6

Graffiti Fight Club

The first rule about graffiti fight club was ...

By now we have all seen or at least know the premise of the movie fight club, an underground society with its own set of perverse rules that governed the darkest parts of our human desire for competition and recognition.

In our world at least, almost every guy and, probably girl, had a thought of making a fist and punching someone square in the face. It's human nature, and I was by no means a fighter, but I have had to step into that "one on one" circle on about six occasions during my graffiti life. I mean, even before that, kids were always fighting other kids where we came from. In our

Catholic School it was common to get "Called out." Quite literally.

In the school yard little Johnny would step up to you in front of all your peers, over a squabble of some kind and declare loudly "I Call you out!" Which meant that after school, or at lunch time you were going to fight. And yes, sometimes these fights happened on school property during the school day.

Why wouldn't they? even if the Nuns caught you fighting you might get detention, but that was about it, it was considered normal for boys to fight each other at this time, by society at large.

It was a wild west style show down, all your classmates who saw you get called out would know the fight was happening, and they would be there wanting to see the fight, the crowd would cheer as tiny little angry fists of children pummeled each other for a few minutes. But at 10 years old how bad was a one-on-one fight really going to get? It usually went no further than a black eye at worst and more commonly ended in a wrestling match in the dirt.

But as we got older, and outside of the areas where you felt safe, the fights had more at stake, particularly when it came to graffiti.

Graffiti was in essence a full contact sport in some ways meaning you couldn't rely on refs or outsiders to prevent you from making contact with your competition. That's not to say you couldn't be a graffiti writer and not be into fighting, such as I was, and you could avoid most situations that would force you to fight, which is what I did to a certain extent.

But graffiti was also a reputation-based game where your graffiti mattered just the same as your interaction with other writers mattered. All your hard work could be for naught if you were to become known as a pussy or someone that wouldn't stand up for themselves.

And by that, I mean, you could never let anyone that wrote or in your neighborhood walk up to you and hit you and you refuse to fight back. You could pick up a pipe and crush that person, it didn't have to be a fair response, but you had to do something. Particularly if it was another writer confronting you for your name or to steal your paint.

In some cases, a disproportionate response, such as the one I just mentioned where you crush your adversary with a pipe was the better response because it would add to your rep as well as discourage others from approaching you in the future.

You could also be in a situation where a group would run up on you, hit you trying to rush you, and you just get out of there without fighting as best you could, that would also be acceptable and that was something I did on several occasions. There was no real reputational damage if you lost your paint in a fight where you were outnumbered so long as you didn't willingly hand it over as a concession for not being hit. These aren't my rules as I perceive them, these were, and will always be the rules of Graffiti Fight Club.

There is no Street Art Fight Club that I am aware of, maybe there is, maybe they have some rules of their own.

Another thing that was not a good look for graffiti writers was to say you were going to fuck someone up and tell people that you wanted to fight them and then when you have the opportunity, not show up. You could not fight as much as you wanted, but don't tell people you want to fight and then not do it. This is a problem that only became worse with the internet.

On three occasions, related to graffiti in some way, I wrote a check by saying I was going to fight another writer or person, and on all three occasions there came a time where someone came to cash that check. Like I said, I had been in about six one on one fights during my graffiti career, none of them particularly legendary, but the other three just sort of happened on the spot and weren't planned in advanced which is what I am talking about here.

Most graffiti writers have experienced this. On two occasions MR SPORTS crew fought one-on-ones that somehow involved me only in the sense that I was friends with him and friends with the person he was fighting, in both cases I was viewed as a neutral party that would add assurance, he would get a fair one-on-one fight without other people jumping in.

Did I mention that yet? As if it wasn't enough of an act of bravado to step up to fight, there was often a good chance some spectator that knew your opponent would punch you in the back of the head while you were fighting the other guy. That is what is commonly referred to as "someone jumping in" and most of us have been there as well. And it sucks.

But MR SPORTS knew me well enough to know that I had a reputation for not allowing people I knew get rushed by other people I knew. I had played the part of this intermediary many times before.

MR SPORTS showed up at my house with Neo RIS one day to fight Kite TMR in Crocheron park, and he did fight Kite, and MR lost and there is no shame in losing a fight. And as planned, no one jumped in. There are actually a bunch of photos of that fight floating around in someone's collection, they look worse than they were because MR had bleach blonde hair at the time, and he got a few cuts on his head that were bleeding and normally when you are bleeding into darker hair you can barely notice it. But in this case the paleness of the hair and skin made it look like he was a bloody mess. But everyone went home the way they came, some a little bruised up and that was part of the game.

Another popular reason for fights between writers or people somewhat affiliated with graffiti was girls, obviously, and throughout history men have been fighting each other over girls, why would graffiti make that any different.

Many TMR kids, including myself started hanging out with girls from Bay Terrace, a neighborhood to the North of Crocheron park, directly across the bay from the Bronx. What girls and who was who in this is not important anymore, but at some point TMR and Bay Terrace boys seemed to merge into one crew, and I swear it all started on a day where I had a "Scheduled" fight with a kid that wrote KD in Bay Terrace.

He was a local writer and a kid I barely knew, but feelings were caught over a girl I was seeing at the time between me and one of his friends and the conversation got funneled down to me and him, and it was set up. Tuesday night at 7pm, meet in the parking lot at Bay Terrace in front of the videogame arcade "Peter Pan" to fight.

I should add, this situation was brought to a head by another TMR kid that was locked up in jail for a few months and when he got out, he beat up a kid in Bay Terrace over this same girl, and tensions from that somehow led to this incident and set fight between myself and KD. Both of us essentially little kids that were going to fight to settle a beef we didn't even really understand, and we have only met one time before.

For some reason however, this fight became the talk of the town. There were two notable TMR wagons or cars at the time that were known for being packed with dudes you did not want to run into, both of these carloads showed up to the fight to support me, which is what a real crew did. But they had connections to Bay Terrace themselves, so they weren't there in a capacity to jump in, just to ensure I didn't get rushed. In attendance that night were people with concealed guns, a guy that just got out of prison for manslaughter, 13 baseball bats, chains, knives, etc.

I make these stories sound funny and cute sometimes, but this was real shit, I mean people died during the course of some of this stuff. But as a kid, and as someone still trying to reconcile exactly what the fuck happened in our youth, looking back, all I can do is be fond of these memories, even though some of them are nothing to be proud of.

But this particular fight was something straight out of 3 o'clock high, something out of Fight Club, it was so cinematic that it almost feels like I'm describing a scene out of the movie the Outsiders rather than real life. But this was real life.

I showed up with my Crocheron crew, who were mostly down with TMR too, but more so were my boys first and foremost. I came with my brother Droma, my boy Seal CWB, and Slaze Bobby-D CWB. Slaze was and is a rough kid, he was a true adolescent at war, he had been in Riker's Island so many times by the time he was 18 that you could see it in the scars on his face, and the scars on his fists. In fact, he is one of the only people I know to do two consecutive 7 months sentences in c-74 keeping him there for 14 months straight.

That was almost unheard of as city time maxed out at a year for the most part. And if you don't know what c-74 was in the 1980s, that's something for another time, it's something we all dreaded, at least from where I was from.

It was 1988 still, we all had that 80s look, the cars were all 80s, I mean just imagine what this scene looked like when we arrived. The four of us pulled up in my brother's car. A collection of stolen car parts from a black Buick Grand National put onto a blue Buick Regal, it was two-tone, someone had carved the word "Thief" onto the surface of the trunk a few weeks earlier while he was in the movies.

My brother oddly thought that was funny and left it there for people to see.

The parking lot was packed with people waiting for the event, at least 40 standing around. The two TMR wagons were circling, I want to say with kids hanging out of the windows with baseball bats, that would probably be an exaggeration, but that's how it felt.

Cars were left on with their headlights lighting an area in front of the movie theater and Peter Pan, both of which were downstairs at the time, this was going to be our arena. When we pulled in, I never expected all of this. I thought there would be 8 of them and us 4 ...I had no idea the TMR wagons were coming, I had no idea every guy and girl in Bay Terrace was coming.

The workers from Jack's Pizza abandoned their stations, they were in the parking lot to watch the fight. We got out of the car; we said what's up to those that knew us. Cro RIS showed up, I didn't even know how he'd heard about it but in his true nature, he always looked out for me. Red was there, Chille, Sent, Rican, all of everyone I had ever called a boy was there to support me. (And probably just to watch me get my ass kicked...)

Stepping into that circle is weird, adrenaline is pumping, but for me I could never get past the surrealness of it, it was so savage, primal. It was so opposite my true character but still it was a calling I needed to answer. I think most people that have never experienced that kind of fight have a small hidden feeling that they wish they did.

It's how the Fight Club gets started in that movie. Brad Pitt says to Ed Norton, "I've never been in a fight, have you?" and that is what unleashed the darkest desire inside of him, inciting the entire plot.

In our own lives, I've said it before, these moments define us, not in a heroic way but in knowing our own spirit and facing the darkest parts of ourselves and humanity. Stepping into that circle to fight, even in grade school, is a defining moment for a kid coming of age. I had done it a few times, not nearly as many times as others, but it is one of the great challenges of adolescence.

On this night, a circle formed, a kid whom I had only seen one time before took off a piece of jewelry and handed it to his friend to hold as he stepped into the ring. The ring as I am calling it was a circle of 40 plus people cheering, waiting, and wanting, to see a fight. It was quite literally a fight club. I didn't know how to really fight, neither did KD whose real name was Kenny. I was about to fight a kid I didn't know and had no beef with, he was about to fight a kid he didn't know. I would rarely ever see him again after this, but the insanity looking back now of trying to hurt someone you didn't know for no reason, what in the fuck was that? What motivated that?

I was Piggy from Lord of the Flies, I was hyper intellectual. I wanted the best for all of us, but I didn't know what that meant. Humanity is motivated by the dark sometimes, I think most times. Previously I had watched Kite fight MR Sports, when the fight started Kite put up his hands and said to MR "You're a punk, what you gonna do?"

I imitated Kite here, this was not my place, I walked forward into the circle and said the same thing to Kenny, he threw up his hands and responded "I ain't no punk" as he threw the first punch, we engaged and threw a few punches back and forth before I swept his leg and he fell back, I landed on top of him and kept punching.

The old man from Jack's Pizza, who knew both of us, had seen enough as he ran in to pull me off of him. My brother thought the old man was jumping in, so my brother ran up and shoulder checked the old man into the crowd, others moved in. Bobby Slaze from my crew now went to what he knew best, he started swinging on everyone, a larger brawl ensued for a few moments before things calmed down.

People were being held back in every direction, Who am I? I thought to myself in the chaos as I accepted hugs of friends who were proud of me. With a smile on my slightly scratched up face, I relished in the moment.

We left, I never spoke to KD again, it was never discussed further, many more fights would happen in Bay Terrace. TMR now hung out in Bay Terrace every night. Did it start with this fight? Probably not but it felt like it did.

People would get hurt badly in some of the fights that would be part of this aftermath, but those are other stories for another time.

For me at least, my childhood did end like the book Lord of the Flies, I am one of the survivors, rescued. I've now transformed back into the child I was supposed to be at the time when I was a pseudo-street kid living this life in a rough city. I'm a 50-year-old man who can finally know what it means to be a child. I look back now and the simplest of nights hurts, but it is not the hurt of regret, quite the opposite, it's a feeling of accomplishment to let human nature run its dark course and be able to survive the environment I was raised in. It hurts in the way all life hurts; all life is suffering. We are the sum of our own experiences, and I am truly blessed to be able to see them now for what they were.

CHAPTER 7

The House by the Park

The house by the park existed in infamy. Everyone in Bayside from near and far knew the house and knew the crazy two brothers that lived in it. Me being one of those brothers.

Not too long ago, present day, on social media I saw a comment from a girl that was considered one of the cutest in the neighborhood in a chat about people they "wished they hooked up with decades ago", and she said "The brothers that lived by the park, oh my ..." or something along those lines.

Wait, what?

My brother and I called that house home from the tail end of '78 all the way to '99, before we made our way over to California. It's wild to think back on it, that spot was my whole world for what feels like forever, yet it was just 20 years. But they weren't just any 20 years; they were the ones where I grew up, figured out life, and transitioned from a boy into a man. Those years packed in all the pivotal moments and lessons that shaped me. Since then, I've been in California for roughly 25 years. It's been a longer stretch, sure, but those adult years just don't hit the same way.

Growing up, every moment feels monumental, but once you're grown, even a quarter-century can breeze by without the same sense of transformation. Don't get me wrong, life continues to change you, and you learn new lessons every day. Some lessons good and some not so good and eventually the weight of life will become apparent.

Our house was nestled in the Bayside area of Queens, right opposite Crocheron Park, which extended all the way to the edges of Little Neck Bay. From Crocheron's furthest point, you could catch glimpses of the Bronx across the Throgs Neck Bridge, and even Kings Point in Long Island wasn't far off, just a straight shot down Northern Blvd.

Over time, this spot would turn into one of Queens' most coveted slices of real estate. But back when my dad sealed the deal on it, we were smack in the middle of the 1970s — not exactly New York's golden era. The city was rough, teeming with challenges. Though Northern Queens managed a bit better compared to the gritty inner-city stretches a few blocks and miles to the south and west, we were still in the thick of New York City's troubles: police misconduct, deep-seeded racism, soaring crime rates, you name it.

The house that would become our house sat vacant for 2 years before my dad got a deal on it. He paid sixty thousand for it, which at the time was just about one year's salary for him. Sounds cheap for a house by today's standards and it was a little bit cheap back then too. The neighbors on that block discouraged buyer after buyer at a time when that sort of thing happened. They wanted the right buyer to come along, my dad being that person for them. In retrospect looking back now I wonder how did my dad earn that much money back then? Sixty thousand is not a great salary by today's standards but adjusted for inflation and true cost of living it was about the equivalent of almost five times that now.

My dad was drafted into the Korean War right out of High School in the Bronx when he just turned 18, he went overseas with the Marines, saw some horrors that would change him forever. He lost some of his best friends, one he feels personally responsible for losing. So much so that when the Marines asked him to escort the dead Marine's body back home to his family in the Bronx, my dad refused, choosing instead to stay in the warzone where he was in Korea at the time. Because as far as my dad was concerned, how in the hell could he face his best friend's parents with his dead body, when he feels like he somehow was responsible?

That is a cross my dad carries to this day at 92 years old. He got rid of all his medals and Marine memorabilia many years ago, just because he thought war was something disgusting and although he loved his country and was willing to lay down his life for her, he just couldn't bear the memories.

It's crazy though if you think about it, now in 2022, more than 40 years later, the majority of the workforce is still lucky to be making sixty thousand dollars per year, and houses in most markets cost ten times that amount in a decent area, in some cities like Los Angeles and New York houses cost almost twenty times that amount for a modestly sized and appointed home.

My dad never worked for anyone either for the most part, he got out of the Marines after the war and went out to California to work with CBS or something and worked there for about a year then went back to New York and started his own printing company in mid-town NYC. And without an education he managed to make a living and raise his family.

My dad was a Frank Sinatra fan, like a total fanatic, he was more than a fan though, he knew him. Not as a friend, I mean he couldn't just call Frank up on the phone, but somehow my dad wound up at dinners with Frank on more than one occasion. At the Copa, in Atlantic City, and so on.

My dad once told me, at one of the dinners they all stood up to take a photo together and one of Frank's guys was between my dad and Frank. They all put their arms around each other and when my dad put his arm around the guy my dad's arm wound up under his jacket which was now lifted because his own arms were around my dad's shoulder on his left side and Frank's on his right. Under his jacket my dad's hand came to rest on this guy's gun in his waistband which startled my dad who had forgotten where he was. "It's one thing to be sitting with guys capable of killing someone but it's another to realize they are armed with loaded weapons at dinner ..." my dad said.

The business my dad started in 1960 and would run for the next 40 years was called ARTANIS ...which was SINATRA spelled backwards.

In the late 1960s ARTANIS would be raided by the secret service with a warrant. It would be investigated by the federal government in other ways too. In a story that my dad reluctantly told me years later, he was an offset printer and as the story goes, a couple of guys used his presses after hours to print counterfeit money eventually getting busted. When they raided my dad's "Shop" as he called it, my dad was ultimately cleared of any wrongdoing and released but they took one of his workers away "forever", and another "fled to Mexico".

It became a running joke at holiday dinners with my "Uncles" who used to joke with my dad - "When he said he was going to stay after and make a little extra money you didn't know what he meant!" and they would all burst into laughter at this irony of "making extra money" literally, the joke of my childhood.

The house by the park was on a block, like I said, that went on to become super desirable once New York became safer, but even in this crazy time in New York it already was attracting upscale immigrant Italians and some Irish, all along the perimeter of the park all the way to the bay. At one end there was a "Yacht

Club" which had a bridge from it directly to the bay and a small marina, and a pool and restaurant and all the amenities that went along with exclusive membership in 1970s New York.

There were only 5 houses on our block, extra wide lots made it even more exclusive, the top of the block was owned by a family "The Tintis" whom we never really saw but the house had a historical plaque on the lawn and was built before the civil war and was the hugest lot on the block. The lots got smaller as they went down the slight hill, with ours being the second to last but it was still great frontage and a decent back yard.

The house next to the Tintis was owned by a guy named Tom Chiesi, but he was known as "Tommy Guns", which my dad told me was his nickname because he had huge biceps and they called those his guns. As I got older though I realized, he didn't really have big biceps, in fact he was quite out of shape, and it became apparent that is not why they called him the Tommy Guns moniker. His house was beautiful, and you could tell he spent a ton of money upkeeping it, it had an amazing pool in the back and he and his wife had two gorgeous daughters.

Next to him was the house next to us as well, it was a "friend of" Tommy Guns named Joe Scorsese who had previously been indicted on tax evasion charges. He was out on some sort of bond when we moved in and I think he cleared it up without any real prison time, maybe he did 6 months or something, I was only 9 at the time.

Joe and my dad would become good friends, Joe owned several car dealerships, and my dad had a penchant for Cadillac's, the large 1970s and 1980s style Coup Devilles, Sedan Devilles and El Dorado styles. Seemed like Joe was giving him a different car every week as my dad always had two or three Cadillacs at any given time. Years later Joe even gave me my first car in 1987 when I was 17, a 1981 Honda Accord hatchback. He gave me a car so "I wouldn't ask to drive my dad's Cadillacs."

I wrecked that Honda a year later when I got T-Boned by some asshole running a red light in Brooklyn Heights. Joe then quickly provided me with a late model Audi 5000 with ridiculously dark tinted windows and it was a bad ass looking car. My image around town now was that my family was rich, and we lived by the park in one of the nice houses.

Joe was obviously connected to the car industry quite well, although I suspect it was the underbelly of the car industry. In about 1988 someone put a bomb in my dad's El Dorado in our driveway, blowing the car up, and when Connie Chung and several other news agencies camped outside our house, they outed Joe Scorsese as a low-level mobster and even went so far to mention my dad and his very Italian name as being "Connected". Which made my dad furious because he wasn't, not really, he was quite law abiding. But being an Italian man in NYC in 1970s and 1980s it was hard to have a lot of Italian friends that weren't somehow connected in one way or another.

That bomb also landed the FBI at our doorstep and the bomb squad vehicles at our house for the next 10 days. You see, when a bomb explodes, it is standard protocol for the feds to find every last piece of shrapnel and damage that the bomb did or left lying around for a two-block radius, they were quite thorough.

The FBI even went so far as to be worried about his kids, us, and they drove us to and from our high school for the next 3 or 4 days, that part was actually really cool. I should clarify, I went to Bronx High School of Science but after graduation I owed two classes that they allowed me to take at Bayside High School. I took one class per semester which kept me at Bayside High School for a year.

The first day we were in the back of the FBI cruiser with the two agents, they stopped at a light and my brother asked them, do you guys have to stop at lights? And the agent responded by throwing the fireball light on the roof and saying "nope!" and then rushing us to school as if we were very important people or something, making everyone stop along the way so they could go through the red lights.

I think they felt kind of bad for us at 17 and 15 years old, you know, having a bomb explode in our driveway and all, so they were trying to be nice to us.

My dad however wasn't having such a good time, he kept throwing agents out of our house and arguing with local police detectives, and when they eventually had a suspect – two 18 year old kids that actually had a vendetta for my brother, my dad refused to press charges and that would create a rift between my family and the local PD that would last for the next decade.

Joe Scorsese felt vindicated when it was proven to not be mob related and he was quoted in a follow up interview with the NY Daily News saying, "I told Sarge (My dad) that I think someone was after his kids the moment this happened!" ...They even got quotes from my mom this time around "The whole house shook!" She exclaimed.

Ultimately the two kids would do years of prison time, we would fight with them and one of them killed himself when he was released.

My dad wrote the Parole Board when they asked for a victim impact statement and cursed the board out saying to release those kids immediately as he never wanted them to go to prison in the first place. Italian Americans, especially at that time, did not have a love for law enforcement and almost never pressed charges or cooperated under any circumstances, it was frowned upon in our community.

It was not something that was discussed explicitly it was just something known, almost innate. If someone was trying to break into your house you wouldn't call the police, you would call your neighbor Joe and Tommy Guns, their response time was must faster and there was much less paperwork. I joke about the paperwork, but that sensibility is something me and my brother carry with us until this day.

If something happens, unless you need paperwork for insurance or something, we called each other and that's how we feel safe. At the end of the day, you can really only rely on family and extended family, no one else is going to go the extra mile for you, but for each other? We will put it all on the line. And this is true today more than ever.

Recently I had a guy in my driveway in Los Angeles trying to break into one of my cars, it was 4am and I happened to be up and saw him on the camera alert so went to look and he was there!

The old me would have armed myself and went outside immediately and fucked dude up, but I had my three-year-old child sleeping in the house, so I asked my wife what she wanted me to do, and she wanted to call the police, so she did. I shined my flashlight on him from inside the house and he quickly left my driveway.

The police took about a half hour to show up and when they did, he was long gone. I was standing in the street when they arrived, holding the large sized "Maglite" flashlight, the kind that police use and often doubles as a club of sorts. The police cruiser, which at this point is a ford explorer SUV, shined their spotlight on me so I put my hands up.

The cruiser inched up next to me. "Why do you have your hands up?" asks the blonde-haired blue-eyed cop in the passenger seat.

"I dunno, its late and I didn't want you to think this flashlight was a gun." I said. As they put the car in park and got out, both blonde-haired, a strange pairing I thought to myself for North Hollywood where their precinct was located.

North Hollywood is primarily Latino, which makes the blonde-haired cops a bit out of place, but that's not really here nor there in the story.

One of my neighbors' cars got broken into before he came to mine. The police told me that even if they had caught him, they probably wouldn't have even arrested him, at best he might have gotten some sort of ticket. The police also said that I had to be careful "handling it myself" because I could be charged with assault if I hurt someone, even on my property, even if they are breaking into my property.

That's the world we live in now, the police are useless, made so by soft politicians and as an individual you are in danger of severe repercussions for handing out your own justice. My advice is having your wife film it and hopefully they try to assault you or something first, then you can go ahead and handle it properly.

Back to Queens circa 1988. After a while the smoked settled, so to speak, on the incident back at our house by the park. There were some lingering effects however, such as our relationship with the local 111th Precinct police Detectives was irreparably damaged; the police for the next few years would stake out my house late at night and try to catch me doing something.

CHAPTER 8

THE WHOLE HOUSE SHOOK

In the interior of a late 1980s grey Cadillac Coup Deville, is myself, my brother, Jimmy, and Alex "Rowens". His last name being Rowens will be a significant tie to this incident that otherwise would not have involved him. He had a Cousin Joseph Rowens too, both of their parents holier than thou and not very shy with the sanctimony.

Joseph was a worse student than Alex and went to a school for kids that had trouble in school, schools like that were common back then, and high schools also had special homerooms and class structures that would keep troubled students separated from the rest of the school, these kids tended to have all their classes in one room with the same group.

We had friends in there, we would often go to the window of these special classrooms, and they would see us, and being that they had issues, psychological issues that were real, they would act up immediately upon seeing us. Bobby Slaze was one of these kids, he was a rough Irish kid, that would be arrested as commonly as most kids would get ice cream; always in trouble and always seemingly enjoying it. He would like to put on a show anytime someone was looking.

This desire to put on a show would cost him years in prison off and on, even back in high school. An odd thing that the city would take a high school student, arrest him inside the school by a city police officer stationed inside the school and sentence him to prison for crimes that weren't exceptionally egregious. But it happened all of the time in NYC in the 1980s and 1990s. It's like you'd be in class next to empty seats and kids that were out would come back after three months on "the Island".

In High School, think about that. Kids were being arrested on school property by a NYC Police Officer that was patrolling the hallways, and we would get sent into real prison and miss school in the process.

And yeah, some of the crimes were real and we have no one to blame but ourselves for that but to get arrested for catching graffiti tags inside a school hallways or bathroom and be sent into the system? Fuck all that.

Bobby was one such kid, always coming back after a couple of weeks or months or even a year or longer. And not long after he'd get back, you'd see written on the walls in the neighborhood "Slaze CWB is back" in black spray paint, like literally the day he would get released. Lacking in him was the most basic human desire to just curl up in bed at home and recover from the horrors of c74, adolescents at war, on Rikers Island.

It was an insatiable inner drive for action that would fuel him. He, and others we grew up with were the real deal when it came to being city kids. As tough as anyone on the planet with human emotions that they could suppress in favor of fun, brutality, and excitement.

That night in my Dad's Cadillac the four of us were driving up Bell Blvd at about 9pm. My dad's plan to not have me drive his Cadillacs failed, even though he got me a car of my own. We took a break to grab some pizza at Pete's, a Greek pizzeria that was a staple for us in Bayside back then.

Pete had known us our whole lives. He didn't always love us, considering how we used to vandalize his bathroom and paint on the front of his store, but he understood we were just kids and put up with it. Years later, when we came back from college as adults, he was always genuinely happy to see us, despite all the trouble we'd caused over the years.

Pete's Pizza wasn't the absolute best, but it was good enough, and the booths had a cozy charm, as beat-up pizza shop booths do. The ambiance was comfortably familiar. By our late teens, it was a place we'd been coming to for years, ever since we were little. It felt like home.

We ate the pizza, drank the sweet fountain coke in the small cup with the crushed us, a slice and that coke was still only like $2.25 at the time, amazing deal even for back then.

We got in the car and drove back up Bell Blvd, checking out the kids on the corners and at the bars, and of course, scoping out the girls while talking our usual shit. We passed by a "Slaze is back" graffiti tag on the side of Carvel and laughed, knowing he was out of jail, and we'd get to see him soon. There were no cell phones, emails, or text messages back then. Seeing his tag on the obvious walls in the neighborhood was literally how we knew he was back.

We drove down 35th Ave towards his house, skirting the south side of Crocheron Park. It must have been around October. My house, directly across the park from where we were, was usually hidden by the thick foliage. But the winter leaves had thinned, making our house somewhat visible through the woods by now. Normally, we wouldn't notice it though in the dark of night, but this night was different.

"What the fuck?" exclaims my brother looking across. There were emergency vehicles and fire trucks and police with their lights flashing at OUR house. What the fuck is right!

Remember, no cell phones existed yet, if something happened at home your parents couldn't call you. You would find out when you got back, whenever that was.

I screeched the tires at the first corner "banging" a right hand turn and circling back as we floored it back the other direction. The engine roared to a scream before the automatic transmission would allow it to switch gears. The V8 Cadillac performing like a race car now, something it always had under the hood but was not often called upon. We screeched loudly as we made the right-hand turn sliding the corners as we drifted towards my block, flooring the car again, the whole neighborhood could hear us coming.

Police were in the streets watching fire trucks hose down my dad's Cadillac El Dorado. We were in his Coup de Ville, but as I've mentioned, he had another Cadillac too. A cream yellow colored Cadillac El Dorado with white leather interior and a dark brown landeau top. This El Dorado Cadillac looked like it was destroyed in a blaze and being put out now by the fire department.

But before we could even get to that point, police drew guns on our vehicle as we screeched up at a high rate of speed. We jumped out anyway. "Get down on the fucking floor!!!" an officer exclaimed.

"He's my son!" Screamed my mom from the front lawn, surrounded by police officers.

Eventually the chaos of our arrival had subsided a bit and we found out that someone had placed a bomb underneath my dad's Cadillac and the bomb went off, destroying the car, starting a fire and damaging the two neighboring houses on our block, as well as our own.

The FBI was now on the scene, news crews, Connie Chung had arrived. Literally.

The initial fervor was my dad being Italian and owning two Cadillacs, our neighbor and his best friend also being Italian and having 4 Cadillac's. Our neighbor was also indicted on tax charges a year prior. There was an obvious theme they wanted to discuss, it was 1988 and this time meant one thing for Italian Americans in the perception of the public. The Mafia.

They insinuated on television my dad was "Mobbed up". Our neighbor too. My dad was confused and mostly quiet now, our neighbor Joe, less quiet, defending his name saying, "this has nothing to do with the Mafia, this has to do with his kids, I'm telling you."

"His kids" as he says, were us, just in case you weren't following along.

Another blast could be heard in the distance, everyone scrambled.

We heard an address come across the radio.

"That's my block!" exclaimed Alex Rowens!

We ran to our car, some of the police ran to their cruisers too. We all sped off together, almost as if we were an unmarked police car in this parade of police vehicles, we all sped in that direction, pedals to the floors, engines wailing to their fullest production of horsepower.

"Pull over to the right!!!" the office exclaimed over the loudspeaker from his racing cruiser.

We had taken the little side road behind PS 41 to link back to 35th and somehow gotten in front of the police racing to the scene. I slowed a bit to allow them to overtake me then floored it again to keep pace racing towards Alex's house.

As we turned the corner, other police cruisers and the fire department had just beaten us to the scene, the whole block was in the street. A bomb was placed at the front door of the house directly next door to Alex Rowens house. This time there was a note taped to the wall.

A GIFT FOR TMR

TMR was not very popular at this time amongst most high school aged kids and even older. You either knew them or you didn't. And even if you did know original TMR kids, their numbers had increased so rapidly that there were TMR kids that didn't really even know other TMR kids, I mean we might have known them, but by now there were rival factions within the crew itself.

The crew were perceived bullies by a good part of the community, major networks had run news stories on

TV and in print with titles like "Inside a gang" and so on, which featured the TMR crew and the vandalism and violence they became known for. In the beginning it was a graffiti crew but out of necessity somewhat it became more of a violent gang to respond to the violence that was prevalent in NYC at this time.

It is a crew peppered with lore and legend, rumors and gossip. One of the main things I get asked to this day is if they were racist. "The Master Race" was literally a concept of Naziism so how could it not be? is what people would say to me.

Of course, there were racist incidents involving a crew of 50 or more people, not aimed at a group in particular but something that happened in the heat of the moment where, in a fight that was already happening someone used a derogatory term. There were a ton of white kids in TMR, but there also a dozen or more people of color in the crew as well.

The person that coined the name of the crew in the first place was Duran TMR, who was not white. He was a comic book geek and the phrase "The master race" was mentioned in a comic episode of Star Trek.

So, the answer to those still wondering is no, TMR is not racist as a crew. Like any other large groups of people though, there of course were exceptions, but the part of the crew I was friends with, were not. Regardless of them not being racist though, they were mean, I mean most of us were mean at some point in

NYC back then. Most crews were robbing people and beating them up, going back to the original graffiti crews of every stretch in NYC in the 1970s and 1980s. NYC was a mean place in the 1980s and 1990s. Kids today have it easy comparatively.

And TMR was prevalent in Queens, particularly Southeastern Queens, they made a lot of enemies. There would be blowback many of us would face time and time again with neighboring areas when they would attack us for things other people in TMR did; even though we didn't hang out with those particular people. We were responsible by association.

There were wagons of carloads of guys in TMR, as I mentioned earlier, that would cruise into other neighborhoods with bats and chains and weapons, like in the outsiders, sometimes guns. And they would "roll up" on other crews and break some heads and send people to the hospital.

One of the funniest memories of my teenage years was going to Cheeky's house to see if he wanted to come paint, and when we got there, he was not there but his mom was. She answered the door and said, "Cheeky is not here, he went on 'roll up'". We almost died laughing.

It was a real thing at the time, a way of life, much as depicted in the film The Outsiders.

One of these wagons, with wood siding, was driven by ROWEN TMR, a notorious gangster in his own right.

Now Rowen TMR and Alex Rowens are two entirely different people. Rowen represented the Union Turnpike and Springfield area of TMR quite prolifically. Alex Rowens was in my crew, didn't write graffiti all that much but may have been associated with "The crew" through his association with me and my boys, who represented more of the Northern Bayside and Bell Blvd part of TMR.

The politics and beefs within the crew were complicated, that would be a book in itself. But my boys and I largely put up the crew CWB almost exclusively by 1988. In addition to a Whitestone crew we were very close with known as WSK.

But apparently someone didn't get the memo. They targeted my house and my dad's Cadillac because they correctly assumed I was TMR. They did not correctly target me for the beef they had with the crew but in my situation, at least they got the house right. But they also targeted Alex Rowens in my crew because they thought he was Rowen TMR. And on top of that they didn't even get his house right. The blew up the front of some elderly couple's home for no reason when they were trying to blow up my friend's house, also for no reason.

Who is they you might ask? We'll get to that.

I can't stress this enough, these were actual bombs, large scale pipe bombs that blew up my dad's car and damaged houses over 100 feet away.

With the bomb meant for Alex Rowens' house they left a note as I said. It simply read –

"A gift for TMR."

THE BOMB SQUAD

When a bomb blows up within the city or state limits it is not taken lightly by the government. The FBI is brought in immediately, and part of the FBI is known as the bomb squad, maybe a bit incorrectly in its inference from the locals but that's the gist of what they were.

They set up a huge truck in front of my house with spotlights lighting the scene to daylight. They will remain at the scene until the collect every piece of the explosive device, even if it lands blocks away.

They will reconstruct the bomb from the pieces, they will knock on doors if they see a hole in windows, they will search people's houses to recover the shrapnel.

In this case my house looked like the center of the galaxy for the next two or three days. News reporters would continue to come around and give updates. My mom would be quoted in the Daily News describing the blast saying, "My whole house shook!" My neighbor Joe would continue to emphasize his vindication from being Mafia by being quoted saying things like "I told Sarge (My dad) the minute this happened, someone is after his kid ..." and things like that.

There was indeed a note aiming this somewhat toward us because we were associated with TMR, but still, the FBI wasn't convinced it was just local kids, they felt like it could be a larger threat to our lives beyond the initial incident. So, they stationed two agents at my house for the two days they were recovering the bomb and doing the investigation. These two agents were to follow me and my brother around as much as they could. Local detectives, who already hated us, would pester my dad daily for interviews and more information and say derogatory things about his children in the process.

My dad had enough of that and threw the two NYPD detectives out of our house in a profanity laced tirade that I have never outdone yet till this day. He continued to chase them into the street and made sure they got on their way with the FBI agents and a few local reporters watching.

Needless to say, these detectives would really start to hate me and my brother after this.

But the FBI agents were far more even keeled. They were nice to us, they would drive us to school in the morning and pick us up after. My brother dropped out of Bronx Science in his Sophomore year and went to Bayside High School, just a few blocks away. I graduated Bronx Science but owed two classes that the school said I could make up at my local school. It took me a year to complete these two classes and I became a fixture at Bayside High School as well.

Oddly enough, I appear in two high school year books, Bronx science as a graduate, and bayside high school, not as an official student but in the lifestyle features because one of the teachers there liked me a great deal. Ed Smith, and he was in charge of putting the yearbooks together.

He insisted I appear in it, and I did.

When we came out of school, the grey FBI caprice classic would be waiting, sometimes even bringing a friend back with us to my house.

The whole experience was quite surreal, but my life was always quite surreal, so much so that I struggle for the confirmation that this is a base reality and not a simulation because after all, how can all of these stories in my books be true? In a single person's life? And I have not even touched the tip of this iceberg. There are parts of my life I'm not even ready to write about yet. But again, I digress.

The FBI would use those rides and time spent with us very cleverly interrogating us without it looking like interrogations, they would ask us questions about everything, they would bring up incidents of violence locally, both in solved and unsolved cases, to get an idea of what we knew. They were trying to gauge what level of people we might have pissed-off and where to start looking. I mean their guess was as good as ours at this point, it could be anyone.

The crew wrapped up after about three days and much to our surprise said they had two suspect they were extraditing back from down south as we speak.

What, how?

I mean talk about detective work, this was not the digital age, everything was cash, there was no video of anything, no cell phones to trace, etc. How on earth could they not only have the suspects in mind already, but how could they have already apprehended them 5 states away?

From that point forward I understood the difference between being investigated by the local police vs. being investigated by the FBI.

EVERYBODY IS BURNING

There was a book by that name published by Random House a few years later in the early 1990s. Written by a New York Post reporter that was from the Bayside area. The inciting incident of that book was this bombing of my house. I am mentioned in the book by name, and it was a book written more so about the perpetrators of this incident, but it included us and TMR in a not so favorable way.

When the police came to my house to tell my dad who they apprehended for this, we didn't even recognize the names. It was two kids, last names redacted from this book, Miguel J. and Michael P. 18 and 19 years old respectively.

Somehow the FBI had started combing local streets grabbing people and asking them what they have heard as standard places to start in bomb investigations, visiting local hardware stores, etc.

They had the bombs reconstructed some-what, they knew what they were made of. Given the locality of this attack directed at two kids in this neighborhood, the FBI knew the materials were purchased or shoplifted locally, they started there.

It took them less than a day or two to get some pimple faced kid that worked the counter at one of the local stores to tell them who they would guess it was based on who'd they had seen in the store.

Don't forget, this incident made major newspapers and got network coverage. Locals were on edge and more so talking about it. A kid that went to Jimmy's high school out in Lawrence had heard a kid he knew telling another kid that some friends were making bombs. I guess he told his parents, and the parents called the police in regard to the news.

Turns out these two leads collided head on with the hearsay of who was talking about making bombs a few months back for something else and who had been getting materials from the local stores.

These kids went on the run the second the police started asking about them. It didn't take long before they were extradited back.

"How old?" my dad asked the detectives in my living room. "18 years old" the officer told my dad.

"Ahhh, they are just kids for Christ's sake, I 'm not interested." My dad replied when they were asking him to press charges, a not so polite conversation that ended with my dad showing these cops the door for a second time.

Through this we now know the names, and the detectives waited for us outside, when they saw me and my brother, they said to us that we were to go nowhere near these kids, they were off limits. They were going to be prosecuted because the elderly couple was going to press charges anyway and they were going to go to prison they said.

Currently they were both locked up in Riker's Island waiting to bond out, but the cops wanted to be very clear we weren't to go looking for them.

What the cops didn't know is that we had no fucking clue who either of them were, but we sure as hell wanted to find out. Not even in some gangster omerta scenario but what the fuck? They put a bomb at our house and blew up my dad's car, they wanted to maybe kill us or at least didn't care if they did. How could someone we didn't know hate us this much?

This changed our perception a little bit, we were on alert going forward in our lives. My brother and I were playing for keeps now, every single adversary treated like a n existential threat going forward. Our crew tightened. Bobby Slaze went everywhere with me; he was ready for revenge even more than I was.

Crazy thing is Bobby Slaze is the one that tells me who they are, not the names, but how we know them. Miguel J. lives directly across the street from Bobby. He lives directly across the park from me! I could see his house from my front lawn and vaguely remember as a kid about a year younger that we never interacted with.

Michael P. lived near Bell Blvd. He grew up with a friend of ours Richie John, he was friends with AZ TMR for fuck's sake.

What was going on? Now we were mad, this was a personal attack, not on the larger crew, but aimed and me and my brother directly by kids that lived on the same blocks we lived on.

That was jolt to our system.

I mean we got it, in the graffiti game and street game in general you make more enemies than friends, it's common for people to not like you, or to want to fight you. But to bomb your house? That is so uncommon it is the only time I know of that it has happened to anyone I have heard of outside of the Mafia.

Miguel J. had a bit of celebrity to him. He had been on the news before, and it was the sole fact we knew about this kid until now.

He had the misfortune of losing both of his parents on a Pan-Am Flight that crashed in the 1980s. He was awarded a substantial sum of money and was being raised by his grandmother or something.

By the time of the bombing incident, he was using drugs a bit, like most kids from our neighborhood, nothing else stood out about him. There was no interaction between us and him.

His relationship with Michael P. remains unknown to me until this day. They were friends I suppose.

Given Miguel's financial situation he was cash bonded out of Riker's Island before Michael was. Long before from what I remember. Bobby Slaze and I were eating at Wendy's on Northern Boulevard, next to the infamous Burger King, one day when Miguel walked in using a cane.

I wouldn't have even recognized him were it not for Bobby Slaze pointing him out. But now there he was, standing right in front of me, the guy the put a bomb under my dad's car, at my house and wanted the worst for me and my family.

What would you have done? Miguel saw us and turned to leave, we chased him into the vestibule and started lighting him up with blows. Bobby had taken Miguel's cane now and was clubbing him with it as he lay prone on the floor half conscious. There were two Harley motorcycle gang bikers in the Wendy's when this happened, the one guy opens the door and shoves us all onto the pavement, he was a big burley dude.

Not sure what his interest was for a moment we all froze.

"One at a time!" he exclaimed as Bobby Slaze took it from here. He proceeded to beat the hell out of Miguel, a kid still I had never seen up close before this day, a kid that for some reason put a bomb at my house.

The detectives came to my house that night, they threatened to arrest me if I went near either of them again, I am not sure why they didn't arrest me then, maybe Miguel refused to press charges, maybe he knew we refused to press charges against him in the first place? Touché if that is the case Miguel, touché.

Miguel would go to prison for a few years not long after that. I would never see him again, he died of a drug overdose not long after he was released. A tragic end to a tragic tale in the first place. The type of thing that was common in our neighborhood by now.

We looked for Michael P. for months while he was out between Riker's and the time, he would go serve prison time. Kids would pull up to my house often and be like "Michael P. is right at old forge pizza now! Jump in" and at a moment's notice we would ski mask up and run into the restaurant with him jumping over the counter as we were swinging on him and chasing him out the back. He was fast though, he always got away.

One Friday night on a packed Bell Blvd. we would finally cross paths and get it on.

It was late winter that year, later 1988 although it may have just crossed over into 1989 by now ...It was cold enough that I had a goose down jacket on but warm enough that it was unzipped. Warm enough that the nightlife on Bell Blvd was packed with people. I was walking up Bell Blvd. on the West side of the street, across from what was Avanti heading South toward 39th Ave. The movie theater was across the street from me and in front of the movie theater was a huge group of kids. One of which was Michael P.

I was with a much smaller group, there were three of us in total, myself, Bobby Slaze, and Jimmy Tame, as we were heading towards Northern to meet our friends Jenny D. (My boy Tom's older sister) and her friends. Jenny had dated Jimmy Tame for a year or so a couple of years back but was now with our boy Alex Rowens.

Michael P. was with a diverse group, kids from middle school 158 area and AZ TMR, amongst others.

"Yo Mike!" I yelled out to him, having still never had a conversation with this person who tried to blow up my house. I got to know him through the times we chased him and through this incident. He had been back in Riker's for some reason for the past few weeks, so we hadn't seen him around.

"Let's do this now!" I continued. We were vastly outnumbered, I didn't really give a shit because I wanted the "one on one" fight anyway, and I knew his boys weren't going to touch me, some of his boys were my boys first and foremost. Which made this whole thing even stranger.

I think BL from Ridgewood was there that night with them, he was confused, why was someone in their group going to fight me? Someone in his crew. At least I think it was him. After this fight it's hard to remember what happened exactly.

As we approached the corner of 39th and Bell the large crowd crossed towards us. Mike stepped to the forefront, AZ for some reason declared loudly "No one is jumping in!"

At first, I assumed he meant that for my protection but later found out he meant no one is jumping in against Mike.

As I was taking my jacket off Mike ran up to me and unleashed a barrage of punches, he was taller than I was. I threw punches back but was no match, he got my jacket over my head and swung me to the floor, I went down between a parked car and the curb, wedged, he started punching me repeatedly, I couldn't move.

AZ again declared "No one jump in!" louder above the yelling from the crowd. Bobby Slaze wasn't having it though, he pushed AZ out of the way and made his way through the crowd. Michael P. was knelt over the top of me continuing to punch me, his head was lined up like a football on a tee.

Bobby Slaze approached quickly like a football kicker trying with all his might to kick a 60-yard field goal. Mike's head popped like a cork when Bobby's foot made contact it was loud. Mike let out a shriek as people moved into the ruckus. For a moment bedlam ensued. Jimmy picked me up, I had a split head with a huge lump, and a concussion. I was groggy.

I pulled myself together and staggered off with my boys to meet up with our other friends as planned.

One of them was a nurse and she treated my wounds and put ice on my head. She advised I had a concussion and to be vigilant for symptoms worsening.

Before long I was drinking beers and passed out.

I survived as usual. Bobby Slaze continued to have my back, and we continued to widen the gap between my closely knit crew and some of our other friends in the neighborhood.

CHAPTER 9

'91 CAPER

At the end of 1990 New York City was as wild as ever. And Times Square was still a shady place you didn't want to spend too much time walking around at night, especially if you weren't ready to face the challenges that might arise.

There was an allure about the city though that often made us turn a blind eye to the darkness and danger. A glitz and glamour admired by the world at large, especially around Christmas time.

During Christmas time New York had a city vibe like no other city I've experienced still. I'm talking about old New York though because I don't see this same vibe there anymore. People that were indifferent or normally agitated at their fellow New Yorkers were noticeably different around Christmas time. It sounds a bit cliché, but it was palpable and real. People greeted each other in the street, held doors for one another. The wished complete strangers Merry Christmas throughout the day.

It is the type of thing no one in New York now but not familiar with New York then would really understand. This was a seasonal thing in NYC back then. Every year the last three or so weeks of the year would transform NYC temporarily.

Beyond seasonal, there were three other notable times historically New Yorkers would come together like Voltron where people that didn't know each other stood in solidarity as something unfolded. Prior to my birth this happened a fourth time I know of, when Kennedy was assassinated.

People stood in front of stores, crying, watching TVs through windows. People looked at their fellow New Yorkers with a sense of commonality that is missing many other times. This I know because I've seen the footage, my dad told me his version of the stories, but I was not there to witness it.

The other three times I've truly seen this spirit come alive, aside from the holiday cheer, was with the 1990s New York Knicks as they neared season's end and the playoffs. New Yorkers thrived on having a common foe, almost as much as they adored their own team.

The city's sports fans have always harbored a special kind of disdain for Chicago and Boston across all games—a rivalry so fierce, even folks who didn't care about sports couldn't help but get caught up in the moment.

Back when the Knicks hit the playoffs, you could stroll past any bar, or wander through Penn Station right beneath the Garden—whether it was a home game or not—and the sidewalks would just freeze. Huge crowds would huddle up, watching the game from a doorway or peering through a window because the bars were too packed to squeeze into. Remember, this was before Google, with no other way to get live updates.

The next time of similar solidarity I remember was much shorter lived. A single evening in fact. The event was the final episode of Seinfeld which aired at 8pm or so, a time when many New Yorkers had not yet begun their evening commutes home yet. If you were on the street around any of the jumbotrons in NYC, thousands of New Yorkers would stand together in the street, if they weren't home, to watch the ending of the most successful television show in history and based in New York. It may not have been filmed in New York, but Seinfeld was as series about New York.

The third and most profound instance was the clearest display of humanity and unity I've ever witnessed firsthand—during and after the 9-11 attacks on the World Trade Center. That day, it wasn't just the

U.S. that was hit; the world rallied behind us, and the nation stood with New York. But let's be clear: New York itself was attacked. For us New Yorkers, it was a direct assault on our lives, our safety, our families, and so much more. Around that time, New Yorkers had little love for anyone outside their own.

You might have shed tears that day without being from New York, but you can't fully grasp that intense feeling we experienced. Consider yourself fortunate for that.

The seasonal solidarity was for the most part short lived, the yearly Christmas time warmth in New York would come crashing to an end every year when the ball dropped on Times Square for New Year's. In 1990 crime was still at a peak in NYC and after a quick belt of the song Aude Lang Syne the crowd at Times Square would descend into chaos with law abiding citizens trying to make it safely out of there as quickly as possible as the rest of the crowd started fucking shit up in no uncertain terms.

Fights would immediately break out, the side streets surrounding Times Square would have garbage cans thrown through windows or riot gates destroyed, fires would be set, and cars sometimes flipped over by unruly mobs.

People were fleeing as much as they were leaving.

We had been around Times Square one time before on New Year's Eve, but the NYPD starts closing streets off limiting access towards the center early in the evening and after certain times the next part of the crowd is kept further back.

So, for New Year's Eve 1990 into 1991 our crew decided lets actually get there early and be in the center of it all which is what the four of us did. It was me, our friend Mark MB who is no longer with us, Jimmy Tame and Seal CWB.

The three of us dressed for the occasion, I turned a goose down jacket inside out so that it was all black and put a bandana on my head, Seal and Jimmy donned black army jackets and hoodies. Make no mistake, we were going there to participate in the mayhem.

Mark MB was from a more well-off family which always juxtaposed with his desire and involvement with the streets in the most comical of ways, at least until it got ugly. But on this night, it was still fun for him despite him not understanding the assignment. He showed up in dress khakis with a boldly colored button up shirt and his hair neatly combed as if he was going to a high society dinner.

We all laughed hysterically when we first saw him, and he got the joke and laughed along with us.

If you knew MB you knew he cared what people thought, to a fault. He was always dressed to impress and always down for whatever, in complete contrast to his silver spoon upbringing and resources. But his dad told him early on he was not like us, and he could never be and that fueled a dangerous recklessness in him that would ultimately lead to his demise, and his dad's.

Another thing about MB is you never knew where you'd wind up when he came to get you in one of his family's cars, often his own brand new Iroc Z28 or his dad's yellow Lincoln Town Car. Maybe his mom's Cadillac or his sister's Ford Explorer, could be any car at any minute.

He pulled up at my house one summer morning beeping his horn. No phone call, no prearranged plans, that was how we did it. We lived just blocks away from one another and our parents expected either of us at any time. I went outside and jumped into the yellow Lincoln, "The stinkin Lincoln" as he called it.

He showed me a piece of green something stuck in between his tooth and gum as we drove away. He had a dentist appointment and that's where we were heading. He often picked me up to just run his errands, but he made the best conversation, usually batshit things on his mind like this piece of green "Reach" floss that had gotten wedged in his gum the night before when he was flossing.

He was furious that he had to go to the dentist and as we sat in the waiting room, he explained how his dentist was going to think he was eating a piece of green candy and that's what got stuck there. Like he was somehow embarrassed that the dentist might think he was slipping. When he instead was the victim of a piece of floss that got him as he was doing the right thing.

The dentist brought us in, yes, I went into the room with them. It took all of one minute for the dentist to stick a little wedge in his tooth and pull out the floss. Mark explained what it was, and the dentist said he knew but as we walked out the door Mark mumbled to me angrily "He thinks I'm fucking lying."

On the way home we stopped for lunch at and got a chicken cutlet sandwich at one of our favorite delis in Whitestone. The sandwich didn't come with lettuce and tomato, but Mark insisted we both get it that way. "Got to get in that extra serving of L-T, you know?"

This is the morning after a night of drug and alcohol abuse that still makes me nauseous to this day thinking about. It was these juxtapositions throughout Mark's life the made it so memorable.
And his outfit for the night of chaos we were heading into was just so him it was perfect.

We got to Times Square around 9pm, it was a little tough already to get as close as we wanted to the center of it all. The police had barricades up and there was a sea of a hundred thousand people already packing the streets. We fought through, we jump some barricades to the jeers of police, we pushed forward like soldiers on a mission.

We had 40s of beer concealed in our jackets and pepper spray on us. We had neoprene ski masks in our pockets if it got too cold or if we needed to conceal our identity. The electricity of the crowd was insane everyone tussling for position, everyone drunk and/or drinking illegally. Music was playing from unknown sources.

People were climbing light poles and street signs trying to get an elevated view, standing on mailboxes, garbage cans etc.

Mixed in with the hooligans were regular people too, people there to revel in the holiday spirit, people that, like us and the rest of the street crowd, were hoping for a good new year. Wanting the best for themselves and their loved ones. We all have that in common and it still hadn't hit midnight yet. The holiday spirit and solidarity of New Yorkers were still in effect for another hour or so.

As the minutes went by the buzz of the crowd amplified, the excitement amplified, it was probably about 25 degrees but not where we were standing. Herded in with the massive crowd it felt mor like 70, we had our jackets open.

Even if you've never been to Times Square at New Year's, but you have gone out, a party, bar, whatever. You know this feeling. By 11:55pm there is an excitement both audible and within each of us. The energy is ramping up, and in a sea of a million people (Was it a full million? I don't know) it was amplified accordingly. There wasn't even a way out at this point, you were sandwiched in. Everyone yelling, cheering. Some MC talking to the crowd in a barely audible sound at this point, the crowd just too loud. The music also drown out by the crowd.

We look at each other, everyone looks at the people they love in these moments, the people you count on. Smiles as far as the eye can see. The pure excitement of life being truly lived is what matters now.

The countdown starts, the ball starts dropping... Ten... Nine... Eight ...

It feels like slow motion as the ball finally drops and we hit the One! The crowd screams, music blasts, it is deafening, you feel the vibrations but not distinct audible sounds.

Everyone is hugging and kissing around you, the traditional song plays and some sing along "Should auld acquaintance be forgot..."

Before the song gets too much further chaos erupts, people start trying to leave and the crowd pushes towards the side streets, everyone wants to move now. The police try to keep it orderly, but people move and run in every direction.

We went down a side street heading east towards Grand Central, fights were breaking out and car alarms set off. You could hear stuff smashing but we left it behind us, we wanted to get back to Queens and did not have a car, we parked it in Flushing and took the train in.

We made it to Grand Central and boarded the 7 train, we got back to main street by 2am and were starving. Before we got in our car, Seal CWB called my brother who was with Paulie Large CWB and told them to meet us at Scobee Diner in Littleneck. We were starving and couldn't wait to get there to eat.

We got there about 2:30am and got a table for the six of us against the back wall. We ordered drinks and burgers; the fries came first, and we were eating them talking shit about the night and having a blast.

If you are not familiar with Scobee Diner in Little Neck Queens, it is an iconic 24/7 diner that is never closed, a slightly upscale diner given its proximity to Long Island rather than the city part of Queens.

It was very popular and was packed at this time on New Year's, every table taken and people waiting to be seated even at 3am now.

Our burgers arrived and as we were eating when we saw two TMR crew friends of ours from Bayside walk in quickly. Image CWB and Derk TMR, and behind them a large mob. Image saw us and casually walked up to our table, pulling an empty chair from a nearby table and sitting down. Derk did the same. It was a bit confusing as our realization of what was going on started to unfold.

They had been at a party a couple blocks away with some girls; this neighborhood is not typically friendly towards TMR kids and has a crew of its own called Little Neck Boys that considered us enemies.

They caught Image and Derk at the party and started to attack them, the fight spilling out into the street and continued for a block or so where they made their way into the diner for refuge from what was now an angry mob. Upon seeing us they sat down and tried to blend in.

The group spotted them and came over to our table screaming at us, our waiter pinned behind between the mob and the wall near our table. It quickly escalated with someone form the mob throwing a glass in our direction that smashed on the wall directly behind us.

Seal CWB was quick to act flipping the table of our food and everything with it into the mob and throwing punches, an all-out brawl ensued. The waiter looked at me terrified and asked me to protect him which I did, pushing people away until I got hit in the side of the head with a glass, I already had a heavy glass bottle of Heinz Ketchup in my hand, something I grabbed just before Seal flipped the table, and I instinctually reacted smashing the bottle over the head of the guy who hit me with the glass.

That Heinz Ketchup bottle is thick, it staggered him backwards and between the ketchup and blood he looked like something out of a horror movie. He took a few more staggering steps before collapsing into another patron's table of food. Customers were clearing out by now.

My brother tackled a guy in the kitchen and fought alongside the kitchen staff to keep people from the mob from grabbing sharp kitchen knives and weapons.

It was pandemonium that spilled into the parking lot with the sounds of sirens heard of approaching police cars in the distance.

A circle formed like straight out of a scene from "West Side Story." And right in the middle of it stood Harry Costigan, son of a well-known judge from Little Neck. He had it out for MB for some reason, oddly enough MB was the son of a well-known attorney. They had history none of us knew about, some Gatsby-esque family rivalry I suppose although no light would ever be shed on that matter. But one thing was sure, Harry was dead set on settling things with MB.

Out of nowhere, some other kid tried to jump into the circle and punch MB, but Derk wasted no time; he landed a punch right on the guy's face, sending him straight to the ground.

Harry took out a butterfly knife and did a kung fu style exhibition with it in the middle of the circle as he was going for MB when two bus boys from the restaurant who, acted like this wasn't their first knife fight, leapt into action. They tackled Harry while grabbing his wrist to stabilize the knife. Once on the floor they did that movie thing where you bash the guy's hand against the floor to get him to drop the weapon which Harry did. The bus boys for some reason then proceeded to pummel Harry into oblivion.

The police, now on scene with guns drawn broke it all up and had us all corralled as they were cuffing us and making arrests. The waiter who I kept safe now came over hysterically crying telling the police that our group were eating and attacked by this mob and that we saved the day. What an ironic twist. In the confusion when the cops asked him to point out who was in our group, he included Image and Derk so we all got let go.

They arrested some of the Little Neck Boys including Harry. Scobee diner was destroyed and would remain closed for the next two days including the New Year's holiday, marking the first time that diner had been closed in many decades.

All Queens newspapers had the story on the front page of the paper, Harry Costigan called out by name with his dad's judiciary identity included.

The case went on to be a black eye on the family and Harry's dad wound up in trouble for trying to meddle in the proceedings as a judge trying to get favoritism for his son.

Our CWB crew had a rap group at this time, it was my brother and Trent who made the beats and did the DJ'ing with Jimmy Tame and myself on the mics, we had a studio set up in my bedroom and we wrote songs about many of our adventures.

This incident had one of the best songs which we wrote the day we saw it front the front page of the Bayside Times. Trent and my brother produced the track, a cheesy Fresh Prince style song, the chorus of which went – "Front page of the papers it was the '91 caper ..."

New Year's Eve Crew 1990 into 1991. Left to right - Seal, MB, Stane, Tame

CHAPTER 10

FIVE MINUTES

I was out on bail in the summer of 1990 from an assault case that I knew I was going to beat; I mean I was there, but I also knew the victims and they knew me and knew what I did was try to break it up. But the victims were indeed fighting with my friends, three other kids I was in the car with, and when we left the scene, the police apparently arrived moments later. There was some damage to their vehicle on Francis Lewis Blvd, and I believe one of them had ended the altercation with a couple of teeth knocked out. It was an unfortunate situation that went like this.

Where AZ TMR lived were these projects looking apartment buildings just behind 7-11 on Northern Blvd near the intersection with Francis Lewis Blvd. I say "Projects looking" because they were not actually subsidized housing, the red bricks and group of them together just made them look that way. There were a few such locations in Bayside.

Outside of his building was an old-fashioned wood fence that was built out of logs, and it was known in the neighborhood as the Rodeo Fence, and its where kids would gather every day, with or without AZ.

There was a younger crew there called DPP, which I can't even remember the original meaning of the initials, but it was a crew of children, and it became known as DPP stood for "Didn't Pass Puberty."

Along with the youngsters some older ones of us would gather there as well waiting for other friends back at a time when we had no cell phones, maybe beepers, but even a beeper meant getting to a payphone that would call back.

Many of the payphones in this part of town at the time no longer had call back numbers on account of the rampant drug dealing. So, there was no way to really get in touch with people largely. We just went to the usual spots and waited for people to drive by checking those spots looking for us.

On this night it was me and a few others standing there when Red TMR pulled up in a 1988 5.7 IROC Z28, in white. We had a coded saying back then, it was "I'll be back in 5 minutes" when we left and only a chosen few knew that actually meant we were never coming back. Tonight, Red pulled up with Chille in the front seat, the T-Tops off and the windows down, music blaring, in the guido lean.

You know that lean, left hand on the steering wheel, arm extended, right elbow on the center consoling leaning towards the center. Looking out the driver window over his left shoulder and extended arm. He says to me "Take a ride, we'll be back in 5 minutes" which I knew to mean we weren't coming back, the other kids I was there with did not. But little did I know what level of "not coming back" we would achieve as it turned into a 2-night stay in the Queens jail system known as Central Booking.

Growing up in New York City's boroughs, a common rite of passage was spending time in Central Booking during nights, weekends, and holidays. Each borough had its own facility, nestled in the lower levels of the city's jails. In Queens, it was beneath the House of Detention; Brooklyn and Manhattan had similar setups, with Manhattan's known as the Tombs.

It wasn't exactly prison, but it had that vibe—far more intense than a quick stop at the local precinct. Typically, you'd spend your first night there before possibly getting arraigned at night court, or waiting till the next day. If you got bail, you'd stay in the system until it was paid; fail to pay within 24 hours, and you'd likely be moved to the regular jail.

Central Booking was packed, with large cells and central toilets exposed to the room, minimal supervision, and frequent fights at that time. I've seen and been in some scraps there, though they usually quelled them quickly.

Back then they had a drug task force, that would raid projects and arrest people by the dozens in paddy wagons and if you were unlucky enough to be in central booking when that happened, it happened to me twice, it would be standing room only for the next

24-36 hours in large cells packed with people wilding and screaming.

In NYC, growing up, winding up in Central Booking was pretty standard, especially for us street kids; it wasn't unusual to end up there a few times. You'd frequently spot acquaintances either already there when you arrived or showing up during your stint, which could be amusing or sometimes just a nuisance.

Every now and then, they'd transfer a seasoned lifer or long timer from upstate to a cell in Queens Central Booking because of some court proceeding, which was pretty surreal for a kid like me, having still not done any length of time. Encountering such a hardened criminal up close was both strange and unexpected. I remember this one time, out of my many stays in Central Booking and a visit to the Manhattan "Tombs," I got placed in the tiniest cell on the far left.

There were a few cells along that wall, most larger and packed with people, but this one was small, fitting maybe ten or twelve at the maximum standing only. Being just 19 and small, I must've looked even younger, and they probably thought they were doing me a favor by isolating me.

Back then, though it's likely different now with added security measures like cameras, there weren't any officers patrolling that back hallway. Once you were locked in, the guards would head back through a heavy door to the intake area, ignoring any complaints unless there was a major ruckus, like a full-blown fight breaking out. Complaints were common in Central Booking; it's many folks' first harsh taste of the NYC judicial system, often coming as a shock. The guards would ignore the cries all night long. And if you were trying to catch some sleep, you'd always hear someone lamenting loudly about being in jail or pestering the guards for something, non-stop throughout the night, especially when it was packed.

Central Booking was a bleak place. Jail itself is a downer. They'd even take your shoelaces and belt to prevent suicides or assaults, leaving you to shuffle around in loose sneakers and sagging pants for the duration of your stay, which could stretch from 36 to 72 hours or more.

The thing was, once you were in there, you were pretty much left to fend for yourself. That day, I was solo in the furthest cell until the clanging of the metal door signaled someone else's arrival. Through the cell bars, I saw they were escorting a real convict, a long timer, dressed in the telltale prison blues from upstate.

His face bore a massive scar, a souvenir of a past slashing, and he was around his late forties. Years of hard time morph people; they age strangely, often looking worn or ghostly. I guessed he was there for a court date the next morning. He just sat opposite me, fixating on me with a steady gaze as the guards exited and shut us in. Those hours dragged on, charged with an uneasy silence, him staring intently, and me, still so young in appearance, trying to evade his piercing look. I kept trying to catch a break, hoping to find him looking away, but no luck. He kept his eyes locked on me. Eventually, I stopped risking glances, knowing he'd still be watching.

Relief came hours later when they introduced a new arrival to our cell, a disheveled vagrant. Despite the stench, it was a welcome change from the intense scrutiny of my silent cellmate. When you are sitting with the monster under your bed, any visitor is a relief.

Digression, as usual, back at the rodeo fence Tommy Red and Chille had just pulled up and asked me to take a ride, said we would be back in 5 minutes. I got into the car in the backseat, of an IROC which was no easy task, it was what is known as a 2 + 2 as opposed to a 4-seater. Like a 911 Porsche, they technically have back seats, but they are small and limited view. I was small at the time and didn't mind anyway, and we all were in the back at some point. Incidentally as I aged, I am claustrophobic to back seats of two door cars now. I mean I guess most adults are.

We drove onto Northern Blvd, and made the right down Francis Lewis, "Franny Lew" as it was culturally known. This is basically where we headed no matter where we were ultimately going, we knew pretty much everyone cruising that strip and even if we were heading to Manhattan, it would always start with a rip down Franny Lew for some racing from light to light, beeping and cheering at people we knew as we raced by at 80mph and more sometimes. Just standard, ultra-reckless behavior, and with all of us, including the driver drinking 40s of beer as we rolled.

We lost a good friend to exactly such activities in the late 1980s. Gary R. who wrote Risk and his twin brother George were two of our close friends as children and at the time Gary worked with my brother and Seal CWB at the Bay Terrace movie theater.

Gary had a red Fiero, which was a cheap Pontiac rip off of a Ferrari, a 2-seater sportscar. Gary got into a street race from light to light heading north on Franny Lew one night on his way home from work. It was something we do all of the time, gunning it full to the floor from the light with another guy trying to race in a rival car next to you.

The pedal would stay down as speeds crossed 100 miles per hour often, a game of chicken of sorts, daring the other guy to keep his accelerator pressed as it became more and more intense. But these were city streets, the intersections we blew through had slopes and curves for drainage, and at that speed heading into a slight bend the car would often go airborne. Even just a few inches are enough to send you off the road like a bullet.

In Gary's case his bullet went right into a massive tree, killing him instantly.

Quite a few people would die under similar circumstances on Franny Lew as it was known. Gary's death is still something me and my brother talk about today, 35 years later. The people pass on, but the memories never fade.

On our journey this night though, about halfway down the strip a car pulled up next to us beeping. It was Robby TMR and a girl, Robby was screaming that some guys just started shit with him and his girl and that he wanted to go get them. He jumped out of his girl's car and into ours as I was leaning over into the hatchback grabbing a baseball bat or two getting ready.

We raced in the direction Robby said to go before coming up on a black mustang. "That's them!" He exclaimed as Tommy Red cut them off and forced them into the curb just north of Northern Blvd. We all jumped out.

Inside the mustang were two Persian brothers I knew from Bayside high school where I had recently made up a class I was missing before graduating. They were with a third kid I did not know. I didn't realize it was them until Robby and Chille were already going to work on them with the baseball bat, destroying their car and knocking one of their teeth out. At this point one looks at me and yells my name recognizing me. I realize now that they are not bad kids, so I try to break it up. Robby yells at me for interfering, says their friends are from Glen Oaks and I knew that if they were all rushing us these kids wouldn't have stepped in to stop it on my behalf.

I didn't care though, I knew them, so I did my best to break it up, but the damage was done by now. Car smashed up and teeth laying on the floor, one of them covered in blood. We got back into Tommy Red's IROC and sped off.

We continued down Franny Lew heading north and we passed St. Francis Prep, approaching Union Turnpike when we saw flashing red and blue lights racing towards us. "Run!" Exclaims Robby.

"It's just because I blew the light back there" replies Tommy, "I have PBA cards, don't worry."

PBA cards were given to friends of police by police officers and contained their badge numbers, I think Tommy even had a mini badge which was like a deluxe card, and if the badge number was a cop of influence, other cops would really respect it, even for minor crimes and just let you leave.

But it became obvious rather quickly that the cops were not stopping us for a light, they ran us off the road, about 4 patrol cars surrounded us, at gunpoint they extracted us from the vehicle, made us get on our knees and pushed us forward onto our faces on the street, kneeling on our backs as they cuffed us. "You still think this was for the light" I said to Tommy sarcastically as they threw us in the patrol vehicles. We were being arrested for three counts of assault II for each of the kids we just got into it with, the police whisked us away.

Normally the ride is straight to central booking or sometimes a pitstop at the local precinct for initial paperwork. But this was a little different. They did not take us to the 111th nor the 109th, the only two precincts with jurisdiction in that area. They drove all the way to Astoria to the 114th Precinct for some reason which never became clear to me.

At the precinct they had a long row of double cells which were all occupied except for the last two in the back, they walked us back and stuck Tommy and Chille in one together, me and Robby in the other and slammed it shut. "Sorry man I gotta go" I said to Robby as I sat on the toilet in the room, "Fuck you" he exclaimed as he stuck his head as close to the bars as he could to breath the hallway air, Red and Chille were laughing and screaming at us, and they started fucking with some crazy dude in the next cell.

They told him that if he took off his clothes and gave it to them by squeezing it through the bars they'd give him something to smoke, but we can't see into the cells next to us, the dude said that he did not have any clothes on and was naked only wrapped in a blanket the cops gave him, they asked for the blanket and he threw it to them, they didn't give him anything back and he started screaming.

Eventually the police came for us and took everyone out of the cells, they lined us all up against the wall, gave the crazy guy his blanket, they chained about twelve of us together by our wrists, the naked guy was alone in his cell on account of him being naked and crazy. The last five of the twelve people chained together went like this - Tommy, Chille, Robby, Me, Crazy Naked guy.

The cop says to me as they start walking us all outside to the bus, "Watch out for that guy sometimes they try to wrap the chain around your neck, stay alert."

Fucking really?

We all got on an NYPD corrections school bus and drove to Queens House of Detention and got processed into central booking where we would sit for the next 24 hours before being arraigned and having a small bail amount of like $250 dollars which our parents posted rather quickly. Except Robby who had already done time for a felony, he had a $10K bail and was moved to Riker's for another day or two before he got out.

My dad came to pick me up and pay my bail. When we walked silently back to the car, he hands me an envelope with a letter in it. It was from the two brothers that we got into the fight with. They apologized to my parents and said I should not have been arrested. They said they told the police that I was a friend and only trying to help. The police arrested me anyway that night. But I knew they were good kids and they stuck up for me in return with the NYPD and Prosecutors.

So, as I was saying, I was out on bail in the summer of 1990 —by now TMR had spun off into two or three main factions and almost separate crews, I mean most everyone was still cool with each other at this point, but not entirely everyone.

There was the part of TMR that was known mostly around Nim's house, this included me, Nim, Voyer, BR, Image, Red, Chille, Tame, Chaz, and a spillover of the younger kids from DPP and AZ's rodeo fence which was just a few blocks away. There were the OG TMR Kids that stayed true to Union Turnpike, and this included Saint, Binky, Johnny Z, Pest, Cro, Sent, Cas, Rob S, and others.

And there was a new part of TMR that was hanging out in Bay Terrace mostly in the schoolyard behind the shopping center. This included TZ who seemed to migrate down there from Union many nights, BL, Paulie D, Victor B, and many newcomers, PAG, KD, JP, Ronnie, etc.

Everyone was mostly cool as I said and often you would see groups from one of any area hanging out at any of the other areas on any given night.

My own crew CWB also had two parts at this point in time, there was Me and Tame, Bose, Jimmy F, Bobby Slaze, Johnny M. Chris Rowens, Image, Gibson Race, and others and then there was my brother Droma's part of the crew, which was him, Goose, Tony Seal, Paulie Large, and a few miscellaneous others. Again, we could all be together on any given night, but most nights we were all out creating our own mayhem in different locations.

Droma was bombing the clearview Expressway one night up towards Jamaica with his boys and there was a Saint straight letter throw up on the highway that had been crossed out pretty vigorously by Fresh Meadows kids. One of them did a throw up in the middle of it and its was lined and scribbled over the rest. Because the throw up was much smaller than the Saint straight letter, the Saint was still somewhat legible, but it had sat like that for a week or two.

At that point my brother went over the throw up on the Saint and crossed out some of the other rival kids that went over Saint in the first place. Droma's throwup was a little too big so now the Saint straight letter was not as clearly legible. Droma put up TMR and TSP in his throwup and in his mind was supporting Saint by cleaning that mess up.

Saint was cool with it, TZ was cool with it, but a bunch of kids that never really went bombing in bay terrace were not cool with it. Led by Victor B they started crossing my brother out and my brother started going

161

back over them, so a small graffiti war developed between my brother's part of my crew and the Bay Terrance part of TMR, while TZ and BL remained neutral saying they had no issue with what Droma did.

Anyway, this went on for a couple of weeks, and like many cross-out wars it escalated to violence. They tried to rush my brother on more than one occasion with him being able to escape pretty much unscathed. And at this point I had seen enough so I became very vocal with the kids in Bay Terrace to leave him alone and back off, it created a bit of a rift between the Nim's House part of TMR and Bay Terrace, to the point that several kids even got into fights about it.

Their fight was sparked by rising tensions from a confrontation I had with Victor B the previous week over the same issue.

Here's what happened: There was a food spot on Bell Blvd called Four Amigos, a Mexican Taco place set up like a pizzeria with counter service and hard laminate booths. It was run by Italian and Irish guys, and felt like a typical pizzeria, but they were serving Mexican food. My brother, some of my crew, and I were there eating—four of us in total. I had my back to the window, sitting next to Paulie Large, while Tony Seal and my brother faced the window. Tony looked up and said, "Uh, Mike (Droma), are these guys friends of yours?" I turned to see the Bay Terrace TMR crew, led by Victor B, signaling for us to come outside and fight—about six of them.

They didn't realize I was there because I had my back to the window, but the idea of them rushing my brother lit a fire in me. I ran outside, got in their faces, and told them that any beef with my brother was now beef with me, and we could settle it right there. They looked at me with disgust, completely caught off guard by my aggression, which still baffles me to this day. What did they think? That I'd let them rush my brother without stepping in? That I wouldn't have a problem with them?

Victor B responded that he was just messing around and was really high on drugs at the moment, promising we'd talk when he was sober. "Whatever, man," I said, and we headed back inside as they stormed off.

Around that same time, I started hanging out with Susan, a girl from Bayside High who was Chille's cousin. She had just started hanging out with the crew, and I was the first one she was interested in, and I kind of liked her back. Oddly enough, we only went out a few times, but I ended up staying in touch with her best friend, who would eventually become my wife.

My first "date" with Susan was a Friday night movie in Flushing, about a week after the Four Amigos incident. Afterward at around 1 a.m., I was driving down Bell Blvd in my Trans AM GTA with her. We stopped at a light near the 24-hour Korean grocery, right next to Avanti nightclub.

There were about 15 kids grouped on the corner—it was Bay Terrace TMR. Victor B walked over to the passenger window and banged on the glass. I rolled it down. "Wanna talk about this now?" he said. So, I pulled over, left the car running with Susan in the passenger seat, and got out to fight Victor B.

I knew all the kids on the corner with Victor B. Some of them I knew really well and wasn't worried about them jumping in, but others, like Cesar Vasquez, who went by Luke because of his love for Star Wars, I didn't trust at all. Luke was a shady kid, only 19 but already in and out of prison multiple times. He was known for carrying a box cutter and slashing kids over minor beefs—a real scumbag if you asked me. I'd known him since we were eight, and I knew he'd try to cut me if he had the chance. Seeing him there worried me, but what choice did I have at that point?

Another kid in the crowd was JT, a good friend of mine and my brother's since we were little kids and lived in Bay Terrace in the late '70s. I wasn't worried about him because I knew him well. But as I was getting ready to step into the circle to fight, JT yelled to Victor B, "Give him one for his brother!"

JT was good friends with my brother, so I glared at him when he said that. He immediately realized how ridiculous he sounded and motioned an apology to me.

A few moments earlier, as I was parking, a green Nova drove by and spotted me near all those kids. Sensing what was about to go down, they circled back. Inside the Nova were two of my good childhood friends, Pete Crest and Jamie Bastille. I'd known them since I was about four, especially Jamie. The Bastille brothers and my brother and I were best friends for most of our childhood.

The Bastille brothers were tough and matured quickly. They had full beards by seventh or eighth grade and were lifting weights like they were in prison by the time we were fifteen. Now, on the cusp of our twenties, they had mature builds and were strong.

They rarely got into fights but often threatened violence, and no one seemed to challenge them face-to-face.

There were some rumors and legendary hits carried out by them in the neighborhood, which added to their rep among those of us who knew or heard the stories.

Jamie Bastille and Pete walked up just as I was about to step into that circle, with my date still waiting in the car. It was a weird situation. Victor B wasn't overly large, and I wasn't afraid of him at all. I saw this fight as a duty, something I just needed to get over with to squash the beef with him, my brother, and now myself. Victor was also close with the real TMR crew up on Union, as was I, so it wasn't like this would escalate into something where my crew and I would really hurt him or rush any of them later.

In short, I just wanted this over with. When I saw Jamie Bastille and Pete, I said, "Don't jump in or anything." Not that I thought they would since they were seriously outnumbered, but Jamie could be unpredictable, and for all I knew, he had a gun on him.

"I'm just here to make sure they don't jump in on you, especially Luke," he whispered to me as I walked into the fight headfirst. Just moments before, I was in the car with my date, holding hands, thinking about maybe fooling around if she was up for it. I was super low energy and not ready for this bullshit at this time.

In contrast, Victor B was standing on the corner with a hyped-up mob, hoping to see me. When I walked into that circle, he exploded, raining down punch after punch as fast as he could. My main goal was just not to get hurt, so I threw a couple of punches at first, then mostly wrapped him up in a Greco-Roman hold. He kept punching, but we were so close that his hits weren't doing any damage. It was definitely annoying, though, and when we slammed up against the brick building, my ear and the side of my face got scraped up enough to draw blood.

I saw his gold chain hanging out of his shirt and, annoyed as hell by now, I snatched it off. "My chain!" he screamed, grasping for it, but not before I chucked it into the street. Things always escalate when something like that happens. The intensity ramped up, and the crowd moved in closer. Luke, who I'd known my entire life, now moved in with a box cutter in hand. He was wearing a hooded sweatshirt, and Jamie Bastille grabbed the much smaller Luke by the hood and threw him into the street like the Hulk, sending Luke tumbling.

"That's it!" I exclaimed as I covered up and stopped fighting. "You got it, Victor, you got it!" It was my way of surrendering the fight. I had no ego in this, as I said this was a fight that I had to have, for my brother, for my neighborhood reputation and to get it over with. Jamie and the others broke it up.

Someone handed Victor back his chain, and Luke, now on his feet, glared at Jamie but knew better. Victor and I ended up shaking hands before I left, and we've remained casual friends ever since with no hard feelings. He lived across the street from my previous serious girlfriend, so I'd known him for years and, oddly enough, always liked him.

I often think about weird chains of events. Given what happened at the end of my first date with Susan, we never really tried again. I stayed in touch with her best friend, though, and eventually married her and started a family. But I wonder—if Victor B hadn't interrupted that date and Susan and I had gone on to fool around that night, might we have continued seeing each other? In that case, I might never have married my wife. It would've been an entirely different life, right? I love my life now, but surely something would've changed, for better or worse.

CHAPTER 11

I'll Always Be Down with the Bombing Scene

In the chapter "Graffiti Fight Club" I referred to myself as a "Pseudo" Street kid because I was, I may have been an actual street kid at one time out of necessity but by 1989 I had Bronx High School of Science on my resume, I had a home where, despite benign neglect and loneliness, I could eat, sleep, and be safe. I also had decent SAT test scores; I had a chance to be the first in our family to get out and go to college.

I had applied to Arizona State University and Binghamton for engineering and got accepted, I was waitlisted by UCLA. I had the options others that had been given the gift of Bronx Science had. I knew I would be going to ASU within a year, so I now had no reason to continue in this life. No reason to be accepting the challenges of the streets, no matter how trivial.

When I was a student at Bronx Science, I was commuting by train through NYC in the early to mid 1980s. That was where I was supposed to be, I had to deal with and learn from that life what the streets wanted to teach me. Prior to that as a young child with parents that weren't around during the day, I also had no choice but to learn what that park and other kids in my neighborhood wanted to teach me.

But what the streets taught me was hard to quit, even with options and no need to continue, I did. What changed is now I would no longer be a true victim if anything happened to me. Some of it would simply be because I made some bad choices.

We kept on racking, we kept on bombing, we kept on fighting, all just because it is who we became, all because its who that park and these streets made us.

Prior to Bronx Science I grew up in a children's hospital for a good part of the 1970s as I mentioned, but those years set me up for all of the madness to come. I would be molested when I was 7 years old in a facility. Violated in the worst possible way and in the aftermath, the hospital explained it away to my parents.

They told them I misunderstood what was happening to me, I was confused. As if anyone could ever be confused about that. I was 7 years old and couldn't play with other children.

At an age when kids normally learn to socialize and notice girls a bit and develop innocent relationships, I was left by myself to read Dungeons and Dragons books, fantasizing about what spells might be handy in killing a certain type of monster. I fantasized what it would be like to kill the monsters in my own life.

By 1980 when me and my brother coded our way into what would eventually become the internet, my handle was Cro Rellik, which was Orc Killer backwards. I had a handle at 10 years old, the way I am @BronscienceOG now, I was already online with a handle in 1980.

My development socially was lagging as I've mentioned. It was slowed, I was way behind. When I was freed, for the time being, of the constraints of my disease in 1980 I came out of the gate unbridled, not ready for what I was about to experience.

My Catholic schoolteachers and nuns told my parents I didn't have the aptitude to take the entrance exam for Stuyvesant and Bronx Science, I didn't have the grades nor the focus. I took the test anyway, I got into both. Bronx Science was the obvious choice for me, my dad grew up in the Bronx, we were from the Bronx; I loved the Bronx.

But my story then is not so unique, many of us had hard childhoods, many still do today. I'm not at all here to say my struggles trump anyone else's. That's why when Eminem the rapper posed the question "if you had One shot ...To seize everything you ever wanted in one moment; Would you capture it?" he became the greatest selling artist of all time. Millions upon millions of children and teens answered that question with a resounding yes, not because they believed they would be given that one shot, but because they needed so desperately to believe they might one day have that shot.

Life leaves most of us hoping for more than what we see out there, and what we saw out there back in the 1980s was dark, there wasn't a lot of light.

I left for college in 1990, I finally got out. When I left New York, I had almost never even been outside of New York. Sure, my mom used to take me to Connecticut some summers to get us out of the city, and I had been to Florida twice, but I had never been west, not even Jersey.

My college applications were, like myself, anemic to say the least. I only took the SAT in my Sophomore year without preparing at all leaving my scores at around 1100.

By the time I should have been taking them again as a Junior and/or Senior, graffiti had become an obsession, and I did not even retake the SAT. My essays were well written, but I had zero extracurricular to speak of by my senior year and didn't even send applications out until I was at Queensboro Community College when I was 19.
Obviously, Harvard was a resounding no. As I said, I got waitlisted at UCLA and accepted to SUNY Binghamton and Arizona State University.

I decided to go to Arizona State without ever seeing it beyond the photos in the package the school sent. My only desire was to get as far from New York City as possible at the time.

My parents packed me up and gleefully drove me out to Arizona State during the summer of 1990. My boys and my girl all at my house to see me off. Tommy D, Mark B, Cro RIS Stopped by, Bobby Slaze, and others. I got into the back of a car my parents rented and drove away from my house waving to my friends and brother out of the back window.

Once I got to Arizona State it was amazing, the contrast of life between 1980s New York City and the number one party school in the country was insane. The weather, the palm trees, the girls and amazing campus. My roommate never showed up to my dorm so I would have my own room for the duration of my college experience.

I started a small crew of kids out there and we got into random mischief on campus, things like turning vending machines upside down and emptying the contents, vandalism, etc. Nothing too major and nothing that didn't sort of fit into the crazy life of college at a party school. I mean there were kids on campus selling every drug you could think of, so I think what we did was rather benign in comparison.

But NYC was still crazy, it still averaged about 2000 murders per year and every time I came home for Christmas or the summer, my brother and my boys would pick me up, paint in the trunk, music blasting and we'd be right back at it, like we never left. Fights were common.

The early '90s bar and club scene on Bell Blvd. in Bayside was unparalleled. Venues like Avanti nightclub and Palm Club, along with a dozen others, attracted diverse crowds that often culminated in massive brawls spilling into the streets.

One year, an of duty police officer got into a fight at a Bell Blvd bar and the guy he was fighting literally executed him right on the sidewalk with a Glock 9mm right in front of the bar and 20 onlookers, I mean the stakes were still insanely high and this incident proves it more than any other.

In this instance, a fight would break out in Palm Club (I Can barely remember the name of the place anymore as it had several names). A mostly white crowd that had the air of a beachfront town bar. Lots of collared shirts, blazers, mixed in with a bunch of drunk Irish and Italian ruffians. A common crowd for Bell at this time, supposing now looking back that we were probably considered as this description by many as well.

During this fight, Patrick Bannon, a big meaty bouncer got rushed by three other dudes and they got the better of him. Furious he ran to his car and grabbed a gun and shot two of them and another guy they were with on the sidewalk. Two of them fell prone, shot. One of them was an off-duty police officer. They were all around mid-twenties in age, incredibly young from where I am sitting now writing this.

Patrick Bannon walked up to the officer and pulled him up by the hair and, while the guy was screaming "I'm a cop!" Bannon then fired a point plank shot into his head executing him.

We were not on Bell that night thankfully, but we had heard the news moments later and rushed up there seeing the enormous aftermath of what happed.

Mind-blowing now, but just matter of fact back then.

The bar was opened shortly after, and Bell nightlife continued unfettered.

I had escaped all of this, but the lure of New York was real. During summers and holidays, I would return home to NYC and away from my new life in Tempe Arizona. My boys were still doing that NYC shit and what's more is they expected me to do NYC shit whenever I got back.

But probably, that's all I wanted too. I say probably because this feeling of getting out was short lived, it wasn't for almost another decade where'd I'd finally be completely broken down by the life I lived in NYC and have to get out for good. Even then, I left with four of my crew for Los Angeles and it followed us there too, some of our darkest days were in our new life brought on by our old life.

There's an old saying, no matter where you go there you are.

In 1991, a trip home for Christmas was launched by the ominous tones of Cypress Hill's "Kill A Man," a sinister soundtrack that welcomed me back into the fold. My brother and my boys picked me up drinking 40s of malt liquor in the car and they had cued up the song for me as a surprise. I hadn't heard it yet. There was no internet at this time, so it wasn't like today where everything was immediately available to everyone.

The drive from JFK to Bayside was a ritual of reentry into a world both nostalgic and menacing. This journey, punctuated by the illegal and the dangerous, was a stark reminder of the life I had briefly escaped but was now, once again, fully immersed in. It was a vivid reawakening to the realities of a city that had shaped me, for better or worse.

Wow, what a fucking sinister song, and what a bad fucking mix of NYC elements, the alcohol, the illegality, the trouble we'd always seemed to be seeking. Mentally, I was already landing back in NYC nostalgic for the darkness of the 1980s which was just a couple years prior, and now I'm handed a 40oz, in a car with my brother and my boys listening to this!

I had sunk back into the seat, it was like a ride out of Training Day, only we were already trained. We pulled over on the Whitestone expressway and did throw ups, still not even home from the airport yet. I was back.

For these couple years every return to New York City thrust me back into its relentless pulse, its streets as violent and unpredictable as ever.

By '92, the city's dangers hadn't ebbed; if anything, they seemed to amplify. It was around this time that House of Pain released their debut album, a powder keg of energy, with "Jump Around" setting the world ablaze. That track, a battle hymn for the reckless, featured in its MTV video my friends and crew from WSK, TMR, among others, brawling during the St. Patrick's Day Parade.

The song became an anthem celebrating chaos and always seemed to ignite fights in clubs and bars with its very first beat, becoming the soundtrack to the mayhem that was our existence.

THE FIGHTING IN PUBLIC DILEMMA

The dilemma is this, if you were to create enough of a scene drawing the police to arrive you are likely going to have problems. If it is just an equal brawl when the police show up, everyone is getting arrested for probably a misdemeanor, but they might put you through the system anyway just to discourage you from doing it again.

Going through the system meant at least a night or two in a crowded jail which wasn't the worst thing by itself. But if the police show up and you are clearly wining the fight, where the other guy is on the floor and a bloody mess, you are now getting arrested for assault. Even if you did not start the fight.

Fighting always meant that in my mind, if I win, there's a good chance I'll catch an assault charge, if I lose, I lose and might get some teeth knocked out or something. Thus, fighting was really a no-win situation in many cases on public streets.

And even worse, (this happened to a friend) something you hear about all the time. In a benign street fight where no one really has much ill intent beyond blackening someone's eye, one guy might fall back and split his head open on a curb and die, and you are now being charged with manslaughter. Again, even if you did not start the fight.

Worse still, as I mention in the first book, you might get "caught-up" when someone that happens to be in the fight with you, regardless of how well you know them or whether you even know they are there. This person might jump into the melee and use a weapon and kill someone and now you will get charged with murder or manslaughter even though you had no idea it was happening. This is what is called being charged for "Acting in Concert" in New York City and other places and now means you are being charged as if you were the one that knowingly and willingly took someone's life or tried to.

For nearly ten years, my boys and I had been flouting New York City's laws with hardly any severe consequences to bring us to our senses. Indeed, we endured some beatings that resulted in emergency room visits, and we spent several nights and weekends locked up in facilities like The Tombs, Queens House, and Riker's Island. A few from our group even served a year or more behind bars, yet it was always considered city time, without the looming fear of extended sentences upstate. This was the case despite our involvement in various crimes and misdemeanors.

But that good luck run was about to end. We were in a bar called XX Roadhouse across the street from Store-24, a 7-11 competitor store that no longer exists to my knowledge. It was about 3:30am and they were doing last call and starting to get people ready to push them out the door. This was the witching hour; this was the time the most beef and fights popped off. The hour when everyone was the drunkest, everyone was feeling tough, and everyone was hyped up.

My inner circle was tight, just a half-dozen or so of us. I'll keep the names under wraps, and the finer details? Let's just say the aftermath of that night's events landed me in the newspapers - marking my second personal appearance in print, but the fifth time my antics caught the media's eye. This was the first time I made the front page though, am I proud of it? Not in the least. The previous mentions? A mix of crew shenanigans and vandalism, some already covered in this book.

In those bars across Bayside, the dynamics were something else – all of us, in some twisted hierarchy, knew each other. We'd band together against any outsider threat from the next town over, a united front of Bayside crew loyalty. But when it was just us, the locals, things could get messy. Nights would devolve into fights among our own, a convoluted dance of allegiance where ego and the thirst for action blurred the lines of community. It was a peculiar, self-destructive cycle, where even within our own neighborhood, anyone outside our immediate circle was viewed with suspicion, if not outright hostility.

And the feeling was mutual; we weren't exactly winning popularity contests. Our reputations preceded us, making it tough to have many fans, for reasons that were clear as day. Even those we hadn't personally crossed paths with seemed to have formed an opinion about us – usually not in our favor. It was a bizarre sense of notoriety, where being known often meant being disliked or annoying someone in some way or another.

About an hour back, "Jump Around" had the club bouncing, literally. The floor turned into a mosh pit, driving out anyone not fueled by a mix of adrenaline and booze – mostly clearing the place of the ladies and anyone else not riding high on testosterone. By the time the night started to wind down, only the toughest or most obnoxious were left standing.

It was common on these nights, particularly like this one when it was snowing out, that you would suddenly hear the smash of bottles in a bar and those bottles would be breaking over someone's head as they were fleeing for safety from a felonious assault on their way out the door. And yes, as I mention, even locals that were known to all were in danger.

As the night edged towards its close, the DJ, in a moment of questionable wisdom, decided to cue up the track following "Jump Around" on the album, titled "Put Your Head Out" – a battle cry set to music. My crew, already buzzed and amped, took over the dance floor, circling up to belt out the lyrics we already knew by heart. It wasn't long before we launched into our own anthem, pounding out "I'll always be down with the bombing scene!" in sync with the fading beats.

Our chant held strong even as the song died down, the music cut off, and the harsh lights exposed the remnants of the night. We kept at it, a defiant echo in the clearing space, until the crowd had dwindled, brushing past us in their exit. Then, as silence took over, we finally let the chant drop and proceeded out the door with the last of the departing hooligans into the night.

Stepping outside was like walking into a spell at first – snowflakes falling, a good six inches of fresh powder blanketing everything. Nighttime snow usually carries this tranquil, almost magical vibe with it, a stark contrast to the chaos of the evening we were leaving behind. But this night, that serene atmosphere was nowhere to be found, overshadowed by the remnants of the adrenaline-fueled frenzy we'd just emerged from.

The scene on Bell was thinning out as folks began trekking towards their parked cars, aiming to head home. Yet, the streets were far from deserted, with a sizable group veering into the 7-11. That's when the snowball fight kicked off, an impromptu battle that saw some snowballs start pelting the 7-11's towering plate glass windows.

Those windows, stretching over eight feet tall, vibrated under the impact, a clamor loud enough to draw the store staff outside, demanding a halt to the snow warfare. But their intervention backfired spectacularly, turning them into prime targets for a barrage of snowballs, hurled with the precision only former little league champs could muster. They were caught in a relentless onslaught, completely overwhelmed.

Normally, some store clerks being pelted with snowballs would be no one else's business but the clerks and those pelting them with the snowballs. The clerks were not locals to Bayside, none of us had any allegiance to them and would often steal from them and annoy them anyway.

But on a night charged with the kind of raw energy this crowd had just spilled out of the bar with? The scene outside the 7-11 took on a whole different level of intensity. You might've thought that local hooligan crew inside 7-11 owned the place, the way they charged out, ready to throw down with anyone in their path on the snowy streets.

The moment that aggression targeted us with violence, retaliation was instant. We didn't stand by when punches were thrown our way; instead, we dove headfirst into the conflict. Suddenly, it was all of us, my crew of six, exchanging blows with about a dozen others right there on the snow-covered street. The scene quickly devolved into chaos, with fighters slipping and sliding, a wild melee spreading.

I noticed one of my boys getting overwhelmed and stomped by two attackers. Armed with "Halt" dog repellent hidden in my jacket, I sprang into action, spraying and swinging to fend them off my friend. By then, the situation had spiraled into utter pandemonium.

"Get that Spic!" one of them shouted referencing me as being the "Spic" that just sprayed them and punched one of them in the face.

We found ourselves engulfed in a frenzied brawl, faces blurring together as we clashed with an indistinct mass of adversaries. It was impossible to distinguish friend from foe outside our immediate circle, with multiple groups throwing down in a free-for-all. Bodies were scattered across the street and sidewalk, a testament to the night's turmoil, some laying on the floor drunk and exhausted, having slipped in the snow. Others out cold or bleeding.

The sudden wail of police sirens and the sight of squad cars sliding into view began to break the momentum of the fight. Some took off running, while others just lay there, defeated or too injured to move. The snow was now marred with streaks of blood, a grim contrast to its earlier untouched state. I was busy pulling one of my friends to his feet, noticing that three from our group had already left the scene by the time the cops showed up.

The police were quick to detain me and the two others with me, just as ambulances started converging on the scene. The amount of blood mixing into the snow seemed excessive for just a few bloody noses or lost teeth.

Watching some being carted off on stretchers, I was caught off guard when the cops questioned me about a knife, snapping photos of my hands and taking my driver's license for record. I had no blood on me anywhere the cop noted. "Blood?" I thought to myself before they revealed that several individuals had been stabbed and were enroute to the hospital, a heavy realization that this violence had escalated far beyond fists and snowballs.

"Holy shit! Stabbed?" I exclaimed, "By who?"

No knife was recovered at the scene, no one was arrested, they took our information and sent us home.

I didn't think much of it and went about my business. A few days later the police detective called my house and said that someone gave him my name as being involved in the fight where people were stabbed.

"Who?" I asked.

The cop told me that neighborhood informant, whose name I shall not even mutter in this book because he is not worth remembrance, said someone I knew was the one that did it. He obviously he had no real knowledge of the incident because the cop was fishing for the name from me. A name I didn't even know in the first place.

Not that I would have given it to him anyway.

I informed the cop that at no point did I even know anyone got stabbed until the police told me after the fight and I still have no knowledge of any of it. They asked me to come in and I refused.

They would call me a few times over the next couple of days and I would not return the phone call and again went back about my business.

It didn't take long however for neighborhood news to get back to me that they showed up places looking for me. I avoided them and was careful they were not outside my house when I was coming and going. Not because I was guilty of any crime other than a random fight, but because I had many prior run ins with the detectives in this precinct and knew how they operated. Shady and dishonest and looking to close cases regardless of the evidence.

They have been giving us a hard time for over 5 years now and locked us up many times previous when they shouldn't have. Even that other night I already mentioned, a few years earlier when the victims themselves told them I did nothing, and the victims left the note at my house for my mom.

The police had their opinions about me and me of them. As such they were always looking for me and I was always avoiding them.

Our close-knit crew ranged in criminality, toughness and involvement through the eight or so of us. About two of us had already done or would go on to do several years in prison. The middle three of us were no strangers to getting locked up for a week or two and often but hadn't served any prolonged time, and the softer more normal kids of our group, the calmest three, stayed out of trouble for the most part despite participating in some crimes that easily could have gotten them locked.

They were just more cautious and not as bold, which was fine with us, they were our best friends and there was no rule about how many times you had to get arrested to be part of our crew. There was however no ratting or snitching tolerated. Meaning that if the police ever picked you up you were never to tell them anything about anyone else, inside our crew or not. Cooperating with the police was and always will be a bad look.

The detectives could not get me for over a week, and they were growing annoyed, so they changed their strategy and went looking for the quieter less involved, to their knowledge, members of our crew.

It appears they had done their homework because the zeroed in on Trent and Jimmy and apprehended both. Two kids for sure that had no prior contact with law enforcement and the detectives planned on scaring them and seeing if they would cooperate.

My phone would ring one day and by now I was answering my home phone in a fake voice, and if it was a man on the other end I would immediately hang up. As had happened before, "Herro?" I answered in a disguised voice. "May I speak with Chris" said a man on the other end. Obviously, a cop, I hung up the phone as I had done a dozen times before in the past week or so.

About 15 minutes goes by and it rings again. And again, I answered "Herro?" in my squeaky fake voice.

This time it was Trent on the other end, "Hey, it's me" he says.

"What's up?" I said.

"Don't get mad at me please." Was his response.

I immediately knew.

"There's someone here with me and Jimmy that wants to talk to you, they cuffed us and brought us to the station." Was what Trent said.

I told him to put the detective on and the detective said he had Jimmy and Trent down there and would arrest them now and put them through the system if I didn't immediately come down to the station and discuss my side of the fight and give them a statement. The detective promised me I would not be arrested on this day and also promised that he would let Trent and Jimmy leave as soon as I got there.

What choice did I have? I called Pat Broderick, a close family friend and my lawyer from that previous case but he was on vacation in Florida for three weeks. It wasn't like today where you could always get a hold of someone, and not wanting to get another lawyer I just went down to the station.

A BAD PENNY

I walked in and told the front desk cop I was to see the detective, he picked up a receiver and said, "Chris is here."

After about 30 seconds I hear in a loud pompous voice "Chris, where have you been?"

Responding to him in the greater sense of where I had been as of late, I said, "Away in college."

"I know that, you left New York but you keep bouncing back like a bad penny! I mean where have you been this past week when I've been trying to get a hold of you?"

He asked that question knowing damn well the answer, I was avoiding him is where I was. We walked back and upstairs and I see both Jimmy and Trent sitting at a desk like orphaned children looking at me with written statements in front of them.

"They can go now, right?" I said.

"Yeah, they can go, they already told me everything." He responded as he gathered their statements and ushered them out.

They sheepishly waved to me on their way out the door. This was such typical cop bullshit too. "They already told me everything." Is a way for them to make you think you have been compromised, in this case there wasn't anything to tell him that involved me in the stabbing in anyway. I still had no idea who was responsible for that, and I was clean of any wrongdoing besides some chaos and pugilism in the street. Maybe some dog repellant.

"Everything they knew" did complicate something for me though. Interactions with the police are like a game of chess, you have to strategically tell them about your own involvement without ever blaming anything on anyone else, and you have to balance making your story believable with information that you know or think others might have already told them. And the truth is I might have gotten arrested for being in the fight in the first place, and possibly for using the dog repellent, self-defense or not.

If you blatantly lie to the police in these interviews and they know you are lying and can prove it with evidence such as other statements that mention you having done something, that will damage your credibility should you later be on trial, even if the trial were for a crime that you didn't commit.

In this case I did punch a few people, not necessarily illegal in a brawl where I was defending myself. But I also did spray people with dog repellant.

When I walked in, there were page long handwritten statements in front of Trent and Jimmy. Did they disclose that I sprayed people with dog repellant? Did the police already establish this to be true?

By design the cop lets me see their statements exist as he stacks the papers up, but doesn't let us converse in anyway before he ushers them out. He sets a piece of paper in front of me and says write down everything I did that night and reminds me that he "Knows everything.' Which is a lie, but he also knows I don't know what anyone has told him and knows I am very careful about the way I am going to respond to inquiries about my involvement.

Seeing as the severity of the ultimate charges for the person they were looking for, I felt it was important to be honest in this situation about my involvement. What follows is exactly the kind of thing that happens when you make statements to the police without your lawyer present.

Turns out I could have notified him that I wanted my lawyer, and they would have had to wait for him to get back before questioning me, but I did not know this at the time. I thought they would have appointed me a public defender and I did not want to waste my time. There was also a good chance he was going to put me into the system right then and there if I tried to "lawyer up," something he threatened me with many times.

My statement was brief, them already having unknown statements from Jimmy and Trent made that part easy. I wrote the truth of my involvement, something along these lines –

I was in the bar that night very drunk, I went there with Jimmy and Trent but saw other friends I knew,(I listed about 8 people I knew here.) A fight broke out during a snowball fight and in the melee, I sprayed a few people that were punching my friends with dog repellant which I had on me because I was an avid bike rider in Arizona where I just returned from, it was in my sweatshirt pocket. The police came, took pictures of my hands, noted that I had no blood on me and sent me home. I had no knowledge of anyone with a knife or anyone getting stabbed until the police told me.

The detective thanked me for coming in and sent me home, that was it.

When I got back to my house there was a message from my lawyer, awful timing to return my call, post facto he advised I not give a statement and let me know that he was calling the precinct today (About an hour after I left!) and informing them I am represented by counsel.

We celebrated Christmas and New Year's that following week and I almost forgot all about this until the phone rang a couple days after the New Year and it was my lawyer, Pat Broderick.

"How is it going, Chris?" he asked?

"Fine." I replied cordially.

"No, it's not." He said.

Funny thing when the police are looking to arrest you and charge you, if you have a lawyer, they will only let the lawyer know, you will not hear back from them. And in this case a few days went by while my Lawyer was making his way back from Florida to New York, he was unreachable at this time. Again, no cell phones back then, remember?

You get lulled into a sense of complacency by the silence from the police or anyone else, you think it went away but most the times it does not. Things rarely resolve themselves. And in this case local officials were pressuring these cops to make an arrest because of all the bad press and violence associated with Bayside.

"You need to go in for a line up." Pat continued.
A line up? What in God's green earth is he talking about? This fight happened blocks from my house, all the participants were from Bayside, why a line up? They knew me personally; how does a line up make sense?

I had never been in an actual line up, like the kind you see in the movie Usual Suspects. Most people haven't. But it was going to happen regardless, because of the pressure of local politicians. Pat told me that he would bring me in the following Monday at 10am, the day I was supposed to be going back to school.

"You're not going anywhere." He said. "Not until we resolve this."

He continued, "These guys are cooperating with law enforcement. You know people that know them, I can't say much more but you know people that know them. You have almost a week, come into my office tomorrow, let's catch up."

The gist of what he was saying is that these are neighborhood guys, friends of friends, all bound by the same code. Why were they cooperating in the prosecution of people in a fight they started? That's not how it works where we are from, you don't get to start a fight, and then turn to the police to punish the people you fought with. Even if something as awful as being stabbed takes place in a wild melee between several groups. And this is what my lawyer was referring to.

He was a mob lawyer, he was a former federal prosecutor against the mob, he knew all too well how this worked. And as I may have mentioned before he hated cooperators, he would not represent someone cooperating with the police either.

When I walked into his office the next day the first thing he said was "Don't tell me what happened, I don't want to know!"

He has never cut me off like this upon seeing me for a new case. I guess the line up was throwing him for a loop too. As a lawyer he wants to fight zealously for my innocence which is assumed (And in this case true). But if I were to tell him I was guilty it might cause him ethical dilemmas when presenting my case. Hence, "He didn't want to know."

He reiterated that I knew what had to be done regarding our "Friends" in common and didn't say much more than that, we arranged for him to pick me up on the day of the line up and I left.

NOT A MUSTANG BUT AN IROC

There was a battle in muscle cars back then, prior, and still until this day. You were either a Ford guy or a Chevy guy, never both. Our crew were Chevy people. We loved Z28s and IROCs, other crews, many in Whitestone in particular preferred the Ford Mustang 5.0s which were cheaper and wildly popular. For the money it was the quickest car you could buy.

We spent many youthful nights in the late 1980s and early 1990's racing our IROZ Z28s versus any Mustang that would dare. Mustang's would usually have us off the line but by the quarter mile we generally edged them out.

Yeah, I said quarter mile, on public streets, on one public street in particular. Francis Lewis Boulevard. "Franny Lew" as it is known locally, is a book in itself, a local writer started to make a movie about it then sold it to studio which made a movie called "Cruise" about it. For me to even make a dent in the topic I would need several chapters, which is not my intent on this go around, for now you can watch that movie and get the idea. We lost friends up there in racing crashes, some of the sickest fights ever happened on Franny Lew and more than anything else it was the pastime of a generation that grew up in the vicinity.

What does all of this have to do with my upcoming line up and potential criminal charges? ...absolutely nothing, other than we had a good friend whose nickname was "IROC" for reasons other than the car. He was getting out of a short stint in Riker's Island for a fight when I heard he was back, and it was about three days from my fateful lineup.

Iroc grew up with and was also friends with the kids we got into a fight with that night.

With no way to contact people, it was a common thing back then to drive by all of the places they might be asking for them.

Trent had gotten a used Saab car that year, the one that looked like a baseball hat. He drove me up to their neighborhood which was dodgy in the first place, because the kids that got stabbed were popular up there and they knew that I was in the fight with them that night, they likely still wanted to beat me up.

For these reasons we figured the new Saab which no one has seen yet would be the best option. I sunk into the passenger seat, hat pulled low and we proceeded to drive around all of the areas our friend Iroc might be.

We came upon a friend known as SB on a corner. I pulled up and asked him if he saw Iroc and he was shocked to see me.

"Yo! What are you doing here? Everyone is looking for you, the cops, (These kids) ...get out of here." He says.

"Where's Iroc?" I respond.

He didn't know so we kept driving around.

It's a weird feeling to be wanted, by adversaries and/or the police. There's a sense of bravado that comes with it, especially when you are living the street life. In the 1980s I was wanted by the local police once for writing because they saw me take the tag near Bell and knew who I was but I got away. And I have been hated by other kids before and had kids looking for me to kick my ass. And in the 1980's there's a satisfying bit of "Billy the Kid" appeal that goes with it.

Even as the police are cuffing you sometimes, it's all part of the game.

But now at 21 years old and enjoying a life in Arizona at an amazing University? This was awful. It was the worst feeling of helplessness and regret for even coming back to this fucking city.

We eventually found Iroc that day and he was appalled to hear these kids that he grew up with were cooperating and going to be picking me out of a line up. "Go to the line up, they ain't going to say shit, but you know the deal, they gonna come for you on the streets so handle it then." He said before giving me a hug. "I know" I said, "Just tell them to stop talking to the police."

I didn't really care about street justice at this point, plus I figured if I could get through this sham of a line up on Monday, I would just get on the next plane back to Arizona and never come back.

CHAPTER 12

ALL COPS HAVE MOUSTACHES

I was 21 years old, but I was still being ID'd to buy liquor until I was almost 50. At 21 I could have easily passed for 17, I had perfect unblemished skin, I was thin and muscular, and almost completely hairless except on top of my head. I dodged the hairy Italian bullet my brother and dad got hit with. The real 5 o'clock shadow and needing to shave.

I shaved once a month if even, I just did not grow hair, and still don't, except for my head which is still a full head of hair today. Weird how that works. My dad and brother both grew beards almost overnight and both started losing their hair early. As if the hair was going to grow on their face and body instead of the top of their head. But I was the opposite.

It was great to have this, girls loved it, it gave me a youthful glow. Great for everything except going into a line up with 5 other "21-year-old men" who all had moustaches and beards and looked 35 years old. In addition, they were all cops and were all wearing the same shoes and pants.

But we will get to that.

Pat Broderick picked me up at 9:30am that Monday morning. I had gotten a bad cold over the weekend and had a fever but was functional. The weekend was stressful because I kept thinking "what if?" and I was going in prepared to get locked up just in case.

I had a very short, shaved head at the time that was just starting to grow out, I reshaved it this weekend. I wore black work pants with no belt needed, knowing if they locked me, they would take my belt, I wore vans slip on sneakers, also black, no laces, because they would also take my laces if they arrested me. I had a white t-shirt on and a black hoodie.

I walked into the precinct with the hood up. I felt sick from the cold and sick from the whole ordeal. I was nervous but was never going to let the cops, nor my own lawyer see it.

A cop comes down to get us and looks at me and says, "He's how old?" in disbelief. You see, they had cops ranging from 22 years old to 28 years old in the lineup with me. All of them with facial hair and looking well into their 30s. The cop immediately knew it was going to be a problem because I looked 16. But they proceeded anyway.

They brough me into a room and stood me next to the 5 cops. My lawyer complained that I was the only one in sneakers and the rest all in the same shoes. The police brought a blue tarp in and had us all sit, covering our legs and feet with the tarp. It was ridiculous. I sat there like a moron with a tarp around my legs, next to 5 guys that all looked like they could have been my father, or grandfather in at least one instance.

My lawyer went into the back, I was shocked already that anyone even showed up to the line up, but I guess a family member pressured one of them to at least come take a look.

About 4 minutes passes before a door opens and my lawyer walks out. He walks over to me and says "You're good, he only picked you out and said you were there. When asked what you did, they said you were just at the fight."

What a relief, I took off my hoodie, sweating from the fever and the situation. I sat in a chair and started to relax when the detective walks in and tells me to stand up I am being arrested!

"Whoa, whoa!" says Pat "Arrested for what?" reaching his hand out to back them up from me. They pushed his hand out of the way and said "First Degree Assault" as they lifted me out of my chair.

You see, they had my statement that I participated in the fight, they knew I sprayed some in the crowd with dog repellent. They were going to charge me felonies for what should have been a minor charge. And they had hated me for a long time, something that showed in the roughness with which they pushed me against the wall and put the cuffs on.

"Put my sweatshirt back on!!!" I screamed. And they obliged.

Pat Broderick stood in front of me as I was cuffed and pulled my hood up before telling me there are reporters downstairs, they are going to do a "perp walk" out of here, don't say anything, look down.

As I said, the police were being pressured by local officials to clean up Bell Blvd, there were murders up there, now stabbings, the press was notified when they set up this line up. And they were making an arrest in connection with that fight no matter what.

I got downstairs and the cops each had me by an arm. There were only two reporters there. I did what my attorney recommended and looked down with the hood on. They tried to ask me some questions which I ignored.

The next day the front page of the Local Times read "Queens man arrested in connection with the stabbings." The article was written by someone I grew up with. It was fucking embarrassing for me and my family. I had nothing to do with anyone getting stabbed, I wasn't even being charged with the stabbings.

When we got outside the precinct the cop says we have to cross the street and lets go of my arm. Anxious to get going I look both ways and just start walking across Northern Boulevard, cuffed. "Hey, stop!" yells the cop as he runs to grab my arm pulling me back to the sidewalk.

"You said we are crossing the street" I muttered.

"I have to walk you, can you imagine if you get hit by a car, cuffed, in front of the precinct."

I shrugged off his lame attempt have a conversation as they finally tucked me into the back of the detective's Caprice Classic. I sat there looking out the window, mad, sad, and feeling sick as we drove through Queens heading towards Central Booking. This was my nightmare; I was going to miss my flight the next day at the very least when all I wanted to do was just get the fuck out of New York.

Inside the system is not where you want to be, ever. Lawyers refer to it as having a client "Inside" as they feverishly work to get you out.

When I arrived, they check you in, take the cuffs off, search you and then move you to the back cells with all of the other losers, like yourself, that are locked up. You sit there a while looking at the rest of your companions eying them and judging them as potential adversaries.

On this day, as I was being brought in, they were bringing my boy Bobby Slaze's older brother out and up to court. He looked at me and called me an idiot, referring to me and his brother constantly getting in trouble with the law. An ironic stone thrown by a man himself, in trouble with the law.

I shrugged it off and did not reply back because he was right, I guess. Not long after they brought me out for my photos, the felony photos. They hang a plate over your shoulder with some numbers and your name and take front and each side view pictures. The quintessential mugshots. Then they return you to the cell.

At some point they bring sandwiches or some crap and pass it out to everyone and you reluctantly eat it. And for a toilet there is just a toilet in the middle of a room of 20 or more people. There are no privacy panels, because the cops need to be able to see everything when they walk by, there is never any privacy.

As the night starts you hope to make night court, which I did not, which means at the earliest I am going to be here at least another 8 hours until morning. I tried to make myself comfortable on the floor in the corner just lying on the cockroach inhabited filthy floor, but you never get comfortable. It's always noisy, people always talking and complaining. New people always being brought in.

Morning court came and they still did not bring me up. Now I was one of the ones yelling, I was demanding a phone call. But before they could even respond they came and told me my lawyer was here and they were bringing him back which they did.

In front of about 11 other people, I stood at the bars talking to my lawyer who was standing on the other side with a cop escort.

"You're being held further" he said. "They are trying to pull some shit with your charges."

He wasn't sure what was happening yet but told me to be patient and that they would be bringing me upstairs soon.

I had no clue what was even happening, it had now been over 24 hours since I was arrested at the lineup. And I was feeling completely sick now, fever raging, having not slept or ate properly.

Another 2 hours passed before we got up to an arraignment court mid-day. Exhausted I stood there and listened to the four counts of assault one charges be read aloud. Then they mumbled some other bullshit to which my lawyer quipped "Are you serious?" to the judge.

If you are ever standing in front of a judge and your lawyer asks for a clarification of seriousness, it is likely not good. And it was terrible in this case.

They were re-arresting me and re-charging me right now in court because one of the "victims" went to the

ICU, that first night. To make matters worse they were citing an acting in concert law because some of stab victims had been sprayed with dog repellent which they argued was proof that I "acted in concert" with an unknown stabber. What they didn't mention was the other 5 people I sprayed with dog repellent in that melee that did not get stabbed.

They wanted me and wanted to prosecute someone for these stabbings, and I was the only one they had. So, I was re-arrested right there for four counts of a class B felony. I was fucked. They took me back downstairs and put me back in central booking. I was charged in acting in concert with an "Unknown assailant" which makes almost no sense.

A few more hours went by, and I was brought back up for night court. By now I was a bit of a celebrity in my holding cell. Four counts this level of charges made me the capo of the group I was being held with. No one's charges were even close, so they showered me with accolades and wise remarks about my appearance and how rough it was going to be for me upstate, etc.

All the things you hope to be teased with when you are in jail.

Upstairs at night court, now almost 40 hours since I had been at the line up, the judge gave me $100,000 bail which was a high amount. My lawyer argued against it, but my name and picture were already on the front page of at least two newspapers. This meant my dad would have to pay $10,000 cash to get me out. Which meant I wasn't going home right now anyway, which also meant they were putting me on the bus to Riker's Island.

The bus ride was surreal. I had never been on "The Island" yet. At least not as a prisoner. Many of my crew mates had but it was new to me. It's a long dark ride across that bridge to 1111 Hazen street, I still remember the address in my head to this day. I did not even look it up, I may have got it wrong, but that's how I remember it.

The cells I was in for the next 6 hours were larger intake cells as I was being processed, then they moved me to a dormitory holding in C-95 or C-76. I looked around at everyone around me while I was waiting, I sat in the corner and spoke to no one. I was scared, lonely and coughing.

I was allowed to use a phone a few hours later and I called my dad. He asked what was wrong because of the tone of my voice. Which till this day I think is funny, and my response reflected that. "I'm in Riker's Island, what do you think is wrong?"

My dad explained that he and his brother, my uncle, had given Pat Broderick the money and he was coming to get me.

A few hours later and I was out.

My attorney was furious with the circumstances as they unfolded, I could barely speak, my fever now 103 and I was shivering. My dad took me home and without even a shower, I climbed into my bed naked and slept for the next 10 hours.

I awoke the next day to my mom telling me that Pat Broderick, my attorney, was on the phone. He wanted to meet in his office to go over my case and explain to me what happened.

Turns out the city was trying to move forward with the case, with the more serious charges even though the kids were not cooperating, he said it was very serious however because anytime the city puts you on trial for something, witnesses or not, there is a chance of a conviction. To the credit of the neighborhood kids involved, they stopped talking to the police which made matters a lot easier for me.

Pat advised I get a job and stay out of trouble for the duration.

I got a job at a dry cleaner that would be starting in a few weeks. I was annoyed at the rules of my bail release, I had to drop out of college. In doing so I did drive back to Arizona with Jimmy and Trent, breaking my bail requirements only about a week after getting out.

I needed to get my stuff from the school and to get the fuck out of New York for a couple of weeks. We drove in my mom's Ford Escort because I was afraid if I bought a plane ticket the police would find out and revoke my bail.

I didn't even tell my attorney we were leaving, we just left. I was essentially a fugitive from justice, at least technically.

The chaos of my situation made the trip surreal; I was Jack Kerouac jumping on the last car of a freight train to nowhere, anywhere. We drove straight without stopping other than for gas, 48 hours or so on the road. It went like this, we left mid-day and stopped in Manhattan for some reason where we bought some new CD's at Sam Goody.

Lords of the Underground just dropped their latest and we would listen to that album ad nauseum for the next 9 days. We drove through New Jersey as the sun set, we drove through the night and watch the sun rise, we drove that entire next day and watched the sun set, and drove through that next night stopping in Albuquerque New Mexico to go to a nightclub and get wasted before getting back into the car and driving again into Arizona.

We were a complete mess of human beings that hadn't showered nor ate anything besides Pepsi, beef jerky or alcohol for almost three days.

Trent and Jimmy weren't in the trouble I was in, but they were involved and played a pivotal role in the dark events as they unfolded. They were there participating in the fight and brought into the station in cuffs, they shared my misery of how it unfolded for me. We were three brothers bucking the system on this trip having left the real world behind for just a week or two of chaos in the face of uncertainty and government persecution.

Stranger still, when I showed up to Arizona State University, I had already given up my dorm room. My mom let them know as soon as I missed that flight that I wasn't coming back. I was already unenrolled and technically not a student. The RA in the dorm where I lived gave us the keys to another empty dorm room to use for the week we were there. The three of us were trespassing on the grounds of a school none of us attended living in student housing, out on bail in another state and illegally there in the first place.

We participated in the dorm life and went to group dinners and other group activities while we were there.

So strange, Trent and Jimmy never even went to the school, and I withdrew weeks prior. Yet in one dorm we were residents and known by all. I wonder how long we could've stayed before being found out? I'm certain we could have made it the whole semester at least.

A night or two earlier, as we cruised through Albuquerque on our way to Arizona, we made a quick pit stop for gas. Out of nowhere, a carload of kids pulled up next to us at a light.

They must've spotted our New York license plate because they got all excited.

"Yo! Where in New York you guys from?" one of them hollered through the window at the red light.

"Queens!" Jimmy shouted back.
"My dad was born in Brooklyn!" one of the kids exclaimed.

Trent, never one to miss a beat, shot back, "I once shot a man in Brooklyn, maybe it was your pops!"

"Fuck you!" the kid yelled, then we all burst into laughter.

"You guys want to go to a sick party?" he continued.

Of course, we did. We followed them to a club in downtown Albuquerque, and the night turned wild. We got wasted and partied like animals on the run, with nothing to lose.

By the time we staggered back to our vehicle, we were beyond smashed. When Jimmy opened the door, I did a front flip into the front bucket seats, smashing my back on the center console before puking onto the street. Somehow, despite barely being able to see straight, we managed to drive another eight hours or more down the road. But we did, and we made it.

The party continued the entire week we were at Arizona State, one night after another, clubs in Scottsdale, frat parties, you name it. We completely forgot about New York.

I completely forgot about being a fugitive from justice and my pending court case. And that was the goal, nothing was right in my life at that moment, but at least it felt right.

Back in New York the case would eventually get cleared after several months and we sued the City of New York and the NYPD and won a cash settlement.

The detectives had no reason to ever charge me with that crime, placing my name and my family name on the front page of the paper for a crime they knew I did not commit. The judge dismissed all of the charges with prejudice, they never should have been brought against me in the first place and they knew it.

The police were found liable in the subsequent civil court action of malicious prosecution and false imprisonment. I never saw those detectives again as the city removed them from the precinct after the court judgement.

Beating the case gave me a new vitality, a new feeling of invincibility thrusting me back into the New York City lifestyle as if none of this ever happened.

It's amazing how easily we move past these periods of trauma and surviving them almost makes us forget them. Time not only heals all wounds it also softens the memory of things we wanted to not remember in the first place. Like the novel idea of staying out of trouble.

CHAPTER 13

FUTURE PRICE SCANDAL

It was 1993 and I had just cleared up that court case stemming from that bar brouhaha that spilled out into the streets at 4am. People could have died, and people, including myself, could have gone to prison for attempted murder, despite the nature of our involvement.

The entire time that court case raged on I was furious with myself, because 1992 was a hiatus year for me now with graffiti. It had to be, I had two arrests and was out on bail from a serious case. All for what? What is fighting? Some barbaric right of male passage fueled by testosterone and beer. There is no point, no possible outcome that is good.

I did the math in my head and figured that even if I'd been caught tagging trains and streets a hundred times in '92, it wouldn't have come close to the trouble I was in. Such a colossal waste.

Facing the grim prospect of losing years of my life for something I didn't even do was a bitter pill to swallow. Yeah, I got mixed up in that five-way rumble, but I didn't stab anyone or even knew who did. Yet, they were ready to ship me off for 30 months upstate for throwing a few harmless punches in the fray. What a world, but that's the justice system, especially in NYC at that time.

In the Bayside area, there was this trio of groups of swanky high-rise condos, each a little world unto itself. Two were smack in Bayside, and the third was over in Lake Success, yet somehow, they were all cut from the same mold. They must have had a common owner, or investor or something of that sort. Each complex had this blueprint: a couple or three skyscrapers linked by an underground shopping strip, complete with subterranean parking.

This mini-mall setup had all the essentials – a dry cleaner, a grocery spot, a diner, and a deli, to name a few. Handy for the residents, right? No need to step outside; just hop in the elevator, hit the basement, and stroll through your indoor mini market to grab whatever you needed.

The spots I'm talking about were Birchwood Towers, Bay Club, and North Shore Towers, each with its own slice of history. Bay Club, quite literally in Bay Terrace, was the newbie, popping up last among them.

All three kicked off construction back in the late '60s, with North Shore and Birchwood wrapping up around '71. Bay Club trailed a bit, launching a year or two later and then, bam, the rough economy of the '70s hit, leaving it a towering shell, bare with no windows, doors, or any sign of life, just stark steel and concrete. A common theme again today with notable high rises in Miami and Los Angeles abandoned and graffitied.

These giants stood unoccupied for almost a decade, turning into unintended landmarks on a landscape of hardened dirt mounds that morphed into makeshift dirt bike tracks and playgrounds for the adventurous, in other words, us. Not just us as in my crew but us in the greater sense of us, incorporating a solidarity of young under supervised children for miles and miles around.

This was during a time when parts of NYC, like Manhattan, Brooklyn, and the Bronx, were riddled with derelict buildings. So, these ghostly towers didn't even cause a ripple in the public eye – just another hidden hangout where kids and teens could escape the watchful eyes of society and revel in their own unsupervised adventures.

The history of the now somewhat luxury residences is lost in the modern world. Only those of us that lived through some of this firsthand have the history and I feel it's important to share with other generations and others from different areas that might know the buildings now.

The three complexes had a similarity in layout and structure with the connecting mall underneath as I mentioned, but it had more in common than that. At least when it came to the dry cleaners.

Now because of the events that took place, none of which are real transgressions against humanity, but still, incidents people might remember, I am not going to disclose exactly which towers this happened at.

During the time I was out on bail in about early 1993 and having regular court dates, my lawyer, the now deceased Pat Broderick, advised that it would be best if I was employed since I was not currently going to college (Because of this arrest and my bail conditions requiring me to remain in the state), or doing anything meaningful.

He felt with the severity of the charges and Grand Jury Indictment coming up, followed by a potential jury trial, a month's long job history couldn't hurt. I should add that the Grand Jury decided not to indict me, because they knew what the cops should have, I was not guilty of the more serious charges.

This was a common practice for defendants, to get employed once they had open cases, it goes with the ill fitted cheap suit when you show up to court. As if looking like a used car salesman with a two-bit job is going to actually sway a potential jury, but I guess in some way, compared to some alternatives, it did and does make a difference.

I had a friend that worked at one of these complex's dry cleaners underneath the buildings. He knew what happened and offered to speak to his boss for me because the dry cleaners in all three of these condominium complexes were owned by the same people. His boss obliged and got me a job at another one of the complexes. For the sake of this book the complex my friend worked at was Complex A and he got me a job at Complex B.

The buildings in Complex B were impressive, towering high-rises.

Looking back, it's embarrassing to admit, but many of the events that shaped my journey to adulthood are cringeworthy to outsiders. Yet, for those in our world —for New York City street kids and 1980s kids in general —these are just familiar tales of stupid adolescence and rebellion.

Sounds like justifications, right? That I am somehow finding ways to excuse my own poor behavior and poor decision making throughout my early life? Maybe ...probably.

On my first day at the dry cleaners, I was greeted by a rather thuggish looking woman named Jasmine and her associate, a heavy-set Puerto Rican girl named Roberta. Neither spoke proper English, and neither had the demeanor of someone who took any kind of crap from anyone.

Standing between them, in complete contrast, was a young, guido version of a Michael J. Fox look-alike — hair perfectly groomed and wearing a collared shirt. He looked like a young Republican, though he was barely old enough to vote. "I'm Sean," he said with a smirk, extending his hand. I accepted it and replied, "Chris."

They got me settled in and showed me the registers, where to put my stuff, etc.

The stores in these malls underneath the buildings typically offered a "valet" service. For the dry cleaners, this meant we would go up to residents' apartments to pick up their dirty laundry or deliver their clean clothes once they were ready. Residents would call us for a pickup, and we'd call them when their clothes were done. We'd load the garments onto a valet cart, the kind you see at hotels, and make our rounds often delivering to and picking up from several units at once.

We had two valet carts, and ultimately, we would be doing these pick-ups and drop offs alone, but since I just started Sean was taking me on his deliveries to train me. Which got us talking, and we essentially spent the better part of the full eight hour shifts together almost every working minute.

It didn't take long in conversation for it to get to graffiti, of which Sean was a huge fan, and notebook ball point pen dreamer at the time. Like most kids that didn't do graffiti yet, he did constantly scribble his name on notebooks and black-books (Sketch books) with his friends and pretend to participate in the culture even without having done any actual graffiti. Sean had very strict parents and as such was entirely a law-abiding citizen at this point in his life. He just graduated high school that summer and not yet decided on, or if he was going to college.

The TMR crew in the 1980s was legendary in these parts and Sean deduced that I wrote Stane and let me know he was a huge fan of my graffiti, and my brother's and Duel's. He found it hard to believe I was working in the cleaners with him.

His excitement fueled a fire in me, even with the open case, that kept our conversations about graffiti entirely throughout the working days. We would sit at the counter in the dry cleaners taking tags on anything we could get our hands on, including the store office binders, order pads, pretty much everything.

Jasmine saw it and said that we could take graffiti tags in the bathroom of the dry cleaners which excited Sean and he ran out to his car. "I'll be right back!" he said. When he returned, he showed me a can of Krylon Ultra Flat Black he had in his trunk, and we went into the bathroom and proceeded to take huge flat black tags all over the walls and across everything.

Jasmine fucking lost it, she thought we were going to take some small marker tags, but we had "no chill" at the time obviously. We made that bathroom look like it was a public restroom in Times Square, which of course public restrooms didn't even exist in NYC at this time for that reason, amongst others.

We had to go buy roller paint and buff the bathroom on our next shift, but we still had the can of paint in the cleaners. The next day on our delivery, Sean shows me the can of black paint in one of his delivery bags while we are waiting for the elevator down from one of the top floors in the luxury buildings. Come here he says as we step into the stairwell and proceed to light it up with the can of flat black, I mean, where was our common sense? The buildings were high security and not open to the public.

Over the next couple of weeks, it got worse believe it or not.

I mentioned this on a related IG post this year. A few years into graffiti, most kids, especially when coupled with punk rock, write all over everything. We wrote on our jeans, our bookbags, our school-books, our skin, all over the insides of our pieces, and around our pieces.

As we got more experienced you realize the less stuff you write in and around your throw ups and pieces the better, sometimes just a single crew is best.

Sean being new and me having been out of the game waiting on this court case for a year in 1992, kicked that initial phase back in. We not only wrote all over everything in the dry cleaner itself, we started writing all over the job tickets, the ones we gave customers, we would sit on the benches in the nicely furnished elevator lobbies on each floor and tag on them while we were waiting, we'd write inside the elevators, etc. It was starting to look like the streets of an undesirable neighborhood in here.

Another thing to note is that while Sean had a clean-cut look, I was quite the opposite. My next court date wasn't for months, and I had pink hair, facial piercings, and tattoos.

One day, a woman walked into the dry cleaner while Sean was helping her. She looked at me and said to him, "He looks disgusting. Is he an ugly girl or something?" I could hear her muttering. Sean, always quick on his feet, turned to me and said out loud, "She said you look disgusting." It was his way of telling her to go screw herself without actually saying it. "Thank you!" I shot back. "Have a nice day," Sean added.

There were several residents in the buildings that did like us though, mostly men, and it was a tips-based job for the bulk of the money we made. So, to the people with the wallets, we went the extra mile and naturally avoided making a mess near where they were.

On older man, a very rich guy was dropping off his dry cleaning one day, telling us they were eating lobsters on his yacht and butter got all over everything, making conversation until the other customers all left.

He leaned into Sean with me in earshot. "They are investigating you guys." He said. "The police and the board."

"For what?" Sean replied. The old man motioned towards one of the dry cleaner's logbooks that had tags all over it. "For graffiti" he said.

That was the tip we needed to avoid capture and almost certain prosecution. We immediately got rid of all the tags in the store visible from the front and never again wrote in those buildings.

I owed that guy a debt of gratitude because had I been arrested while on bail for the more serious case, at the job I had for court reasons in the first place, they might have revoked my bail and locked me up for the next 6 months until the case was resolved. And from lock up the deals they offer get worse, and the chances at winning a jury trial get worse.

But that fear of escaping a close one didn't last long, back then we might have called it boys will be boys, today I would call it a character flaw possibly, but we moved on immediately to something else, and of course illegal.

In the movie Office Space they refer to a legendary scam where they cook the computer code to skim a fraction of a cent off of partial sales prices that fluctuate of stocks or some sort of commodities, the idea being that no one will even notice the missing ¼ of a penny but if you do this a million times per day by the end of the year you have millions of dollars.

Oddly enough this is how companies like Robinhood that do "free trades" make their money today, it's completely legal the way they do it, they execute a trade at an intended price in your order and always return you a price that was affected by "real time" fluctuations with them nabbing a few cents or more in either direction. They literally skim our money right in front of us and we say thank you.

In the dry-cleaning business, there was a similar scam, or so the story goes. Another legendary one, like in the movie Office Space that no one has ever done, but if they did do it, it would go like this.

THE SCANDAL

Was it really a character flaw? I don't know, I doubt it. The stuff we did, and even worse, was so common in New York City during the 1980s and 1990s. I know kids who went on to graduate from Ivy League colleges who were running employee theft rings from their holiday jobs while home on winter break.

I think money was so scarce for most of us in the 1980s and 1990s that the consensus was most city kids and even not city kids were always on the lookout for ways to get over on the system, to make money and more money anyway you could. I mean we all knew kids that did stick ups and armed robberies, so most of what we did was rather soft comparably, although we did cross the line at times, stories for the third book perhaps.

One of the things about memoirs and writing, in general, is that if you're only going to tell the good parts of your history, don't bother—no one cares. Most people have some darkness inside.

The city was dark at this time, with little hope for a future, coming from homes that never saw college. Our dads worked menial jobs 12 hours a day just to keep us going and out of trouble as best they could. And we were the lucky ones. Whole segments of the city had it far worse than us. They participated in similar activities and worse, but what choice did they or we have?

We transgressed against society, often. And I look at society today and still think it sucks for the most part, in many ways its worse.

One of the services the dry cleaner provided was tailoring, custom work that we would often take in when the tailor was not there. He worked only three days per week, but people dropped off tailoring every day. Sean and I knew how to mark and pin the hem or waist and give them a receipt. But one thing we could not give them was a price, so the receipt was a partial little tear off tag from a future receipt that would match the number at pick up and payment time.

We could never steal from the register under normal circumstances because the register was computerized, and it tallied the business. But when you took in tailoring there was a key called "Future

Price" meaning that it would be entered into the system in the future and the system had no way to know what that price would be in another week.

When the tailor was done with the clothes, he would hang them on the rack and hand write the price for the work on a paper ticket that we would then enter into the computer register under the original ticket number and now it would print out the receipt like any other job as if that price was entered at the original drop off.

If it was a $30 hem it was now a $5 hem and so on. So, when the customer picked it up we would tell them it was $30 showing them the handwritten ticket and take the cash. But we entered only the $5 amount in the system. At the end of the night the register would close out with the amount of the receipts from the day and any overage would be ours. Or we might just pull it out right after they left, there were no cameras or anything.

The tailor was busy too so there was a lot of work which meant a lot of money. It became known as the future price scandal amongst us. On larger tailor jobs we would literally race each other to the counter, sometimes jumping over the counter to grab the order so that we could ring it up and take the whole score, essentially snookering the other out of the money.

It added to the excitement and created a very weird atmosphere I'm sure when the customers saw the enthusiasm with which we leapt up and over the counter to help them.

At the time, we never considered who was eating those losses. Was it the tailor himself who didn't record his own prices into a logbook? Likely, he'd lose track of the amount, and the register would only track what we entered. He was probably coming up short a large sum every two weeks, but that's not likely, he would have known.

More likely the accountant of the dry cleaner wasn't cross-checking the bills the tailor gave the dry cleaner with the actual prices entered into the system. I'd assume it was the latter because the tailor always seemed happy, and the dry cleaner was owned by people we never saw who owned many dry cleaners. Their shortfall would be significantly less impactful. And that's how I would've justified it to myself if this really happened, like in the movie Office Space.

GET A REAL BIKE

Things were going smoothly for many months of this and then one day ...I know what you're thinking, no we didn't get caught.

Someone walked into the shop that would change things forever, bringing so much heat that we couldn't risk him finding out.

In the first book I mentioned Andy, he was a blue collar family kid that happened to grow up next door to Alex Rowens, not the house next door that got pipe bombed but on the other side. His family were seemingly good people, and probably were but young Andy would have a penchant for getting in trouble and being extremely reckless.

He used to make the robotic voice and constantly jab at people saying things like "MMMMM ...G et a REEEEAAAAAL BIKE ...referring to other kids BMX bikes. And when it came to stunts, his jumps were always higher than everyone else's, his table tops always flatter. His recklessness in life made him an impressive BMX bike rider when it came to hitting local jumps and hazards where we lived.

His reckless streak and penchant for trouble would often get him in trouble and suspended from our Catholic school and would lead him, where that kind of behavior usually leads, to drugs at an early age. By the time he was 16 years old he was addicted to, the pandemic of most major cities in the 1980s, crack cocaine.

This would further lead him down the path of robberies and stealing cars and he would often pick me up by 1988 to drive me to Bayside High School, where I was making up the two classes from Bronx Science post-graduation.

Andy was not attending school at this time as his drug addiction was messing his life up bad. And when I say he used to pick me up in the morning to drive me to school every day, I mean he picked me up in cars he stole and had been driving around with high on drugs since the night before. And for some reason and lack of a better judgement from me at the time, I would get in every morning for a quick ride before he dropped me off and made a scene in his exodus.

As I did mention in the first book, New York City Prose, he did crash into a car leaving a local nightclub early morning one day while evading the police. Inside the car were two young girls leaving the nightclub and one of them was killed in the crash, resulting in his arrest and imprisonment.

He would go on to serve 4 years out of a 10-year sentence upstate before being released through a half-way house under the stipulation he had to be gainfully employed. By some twist of fate, he found himself employed at the same dry cleaners where I was working, also as part of a court release.

FROZEN IN TIME

If you've ever known someone that did years in an upstate prison, or done the years yourself, it is a bit like being placed in a time capsule, meaning that when you get out, you think the world is the same as the world was when you left. You expect the music to be the same, the styles of clothing to be the same, etc.

Often if you see one of these individuals, they stand out a bit, their hairstyle is a blast from the past, their jeans, the music they like and more. In this case 4 years might not seem like a long time, but in the transition between 1988 and 1992 it was rather noticeable. The end of the 1980s freestyle music and hip-hop street look ran head on into grunge and clubs and the contrast was remarkable.

One day early in our shift at the drycleaners, Sean and I are sitting at the counter looking out into the mall hallway at people walk past when into our view walks a dude dressed about 5 years prior, champion sweatshirt over a white mock neck, hair slicked back with a tail, and a gold chain.

He immediately catches our eye, but I don't immediately recognize him. He is almost passed the cleaners when he snaps and looks up realizing he almost passed it. He steps back and enters. Before he could even say what he was about to say he sees me and recognizes me, catching both of us completely by surprise.

"Yoooo, what's up!" he says to me. "Oh my god" I reply as I get up to shake his hand and we pull each other into a hug. "Haven't seen you in a minute!" I exclaim. "You good? You out?" I continue.
He goes on to tell me he is in a halfway house on work release, Sean is completely confused which I realize and then make the introduction.

"So, you are working in these buildings?" I ask.

"I'm working at this dry cleaners!" He exclaims with excitement. The look of shock on my face was palpable to Sean who still didn't have a clue who he was besides the basic name introduction.

"Chris, you want to do that 14 Oscar delivery now?" Sean says. Clearly, we didn't still do deliveries together at this point, but Sean really wanted to know what was happening. 14 Oscar itself was funny to us. There was this old war vet that lived in one of the buildings. He was a successful businessman now but still used the military phonetic alphabet when he called and spoke to us. He lived in condo 14-O, so every time he called down, he would say "Fourteen Oscar" in a very official sounding voice, a joke me and Sean still make together till this day.

Andy asked for Roberta the manager and we got them introduced and then we left on our pretend delivery when I explained to Sean the whole story. Obviously, Sean was familiar with that story but was shocked because he had never met anyone that had done prison time before.

And the party as we knew it would be over at the cleaners for the near future anyway, because with Andy came some heat, and with the heat the atmosphere around there was thick.

It wasn't two days later that he and Sean walked to the diner in the mall to pick up our lunch when they returned Andy pulled something from his jacket. "Bleaw!!!!" he exclaimed as he pulled out the UNICEF collection jar that sat next to the register in the diner. It was always filled with cash donations.

As you could probably imagine, he didn't last long at work, he relapsed into addiction and his old ways and stopped coming not long after. But Sean would bring up that theft of the UNICEF jar often saying how he could never steal anything.

This conversation shifted towards graffiti, and I told him that if he ever did graffiti, if my case was ever cleared up, he would have to steal spray paint. "Never!" he said.

But I explained to him it was absolutely necessary and if he wanted to participate in my post case comeback, should I be so lucky, that I would not bomb with him if he was buying paint. He still refused and reiterated that he could not.

I simply said, "You can, and you will." And we left it at that. I mean he was already caught up in the future price scandal, surely the transgression of shoplifting paint was even lower on the criminality scale than that.

But for some that feeling of concealing something in a store and walking out with it is just too much pressure; Right or wrong is secondary to the actual pressure of doing so.

Without getting into the details of what happened with my case, suffice it to say that through a series of negotiations with people in the neighborhood the kids decided to stop pressing charges which they had to anyway because they knew I didn't have anything to do with them getting stabbed. I was cleared, and case dismissed.

My lawyer would launch a successful lawsuit against the NYPD and City of New York for malicious prosecution and false imprisonment, damage to reputation, etc. The incoming cash award was great, but it was my freedom to do what I wanted again that was the best part.

I still had some cans but as soon as my brother got home for Spring break a month later, we would start racking all over again getting ready for our comeback.

I spotted Sean a couple cans one night after work and we went and did some throw-ups on the grand central parkway service road. He was immediately addicted, as was I, like a junkie back on the junk.

Another friend of mine was wanting to go bombing and do pieces now too. It was a younger kid from the neighborhood and someone we were very close with Tommy D. I had known Tommy since he was in a stroller because his sister and I went to Catholic school together for 8 years. He was almost 5 years younger than me, but we became close after the death of his father through skateboarding, basketball, and now graffiti.

I told him the same thing I told Sean, you need to go racking and steal paint if you want to do this.

Better yet I said to both of them, you guys need to go racking together, and when you get 30 cans each we can start.

Sean continued his refusal for another day or so before he finally answered that phone call from Tommy D. and went racking. They, like most of us found it addicting and they would rack hundreds of cans by the summer of 1993.

Along with being racking partners, Sean and Tom started bombing in the neighborhood together, leading to a fateful beef that would unite the two top crews from our area of Bayside.

CHAPTER 14

THERE ARE NO RULES

There has long been rumor of an unwritten "rule" of graffiti, a hierarchy if you will, about what "content" for lack of a better word, was able to go over what other content. The common thought was "Pieces" could go over "Throw-ups", and throw-ups could go over "Tags", the result of which would be accepted by the graffiti community as no sign of disrespect.

But as I've said many times, there is no honor amongst thieves and there are no rules in graffiti. If you cover up something someone else painted and they realize it, it's up to them to decide if you going over their tag or throw up with your piece is acceptable. Many times, people got mad and punched someone in the face anyway, because there are no fucking rules in graffiti. You can write anywhere and over anything you want, but you had better be prepared to face the consequences if the streets come calling.

Tommy D. went to St. Francis Prep High School with a kid that wrote VOR DBI, a well-known writer in our part of town in the early stages of his becoming a well-known writer throughout NYC. His primary partner at the time was DEAD DBI. Tommy knew VOR remotely, but not really. Tommy played varsity basketball and football at one point, was a bit of a jock, while VOR, like most of the DBI crew and many of my own crew were not into sports and into art and comics and chess and things that would be considered nerdy in most circles of "cool" high school kids.

Our crew had a lot in common with the DBI crew, but we didn't know it yet.

On a side street in Bayside, 35th Ave. there was a block of stores surrounded by the houses and apartment buildings of the neighborhood. There were only three or four stores in this tiny enclave of retail amongst all the residential. And they had silver riot gates that were not covered in graffiti because it was an out of the way area and most writers would never find themselves on this remote street. Except it happened to be two blocks from where VOR lived and about two blocks from where Tommy lived. Tom was the first to hit the gates and took large TOM CWB tags across the entirety of each gate. Just tags, in black.

Not long after, maybe inspired by seeing the graffiti on the gates by Tom, Vor decided to do fill in throw ups across the gates. Using the common thought that throw-ups go over tags as justification. There was no beef intended by Vor.

But Duel and I didn't see it that way, Tom had those gates prominently displayed with our crew and his tag and it was a street we drove by often, so seeing our crew and mate up became part of our daily routine. Then all of the sudden the gates no longer represented us, but another writer and another crew.

Duel questioned Tom about it and Tom decided to go back to the gates and go over Vor, which he did. Vor then went back over it and voila! A war was born. Tom and Vor now officially had beef.

It was a very minor thing really, a couple of kids that just finished high school beefing over a gate or two on a block that no real NYC writers were probably ever going to see. But that's not how graffiti works, doesn't really matter how inconspicuous of a spot it is or if it was just a tag, the feelings are real.

And with the teasing of older writers like Duel and myself, it blossomed into a nice little war between the two before it came to a head one night when we ran into Cuba DBI. We had just come from Duel's house coincidentally, and Duel was giving it to Tom pretty good, saying it didn't really matter because the beef between Tom and Vor was a "toy dispute" and neither of them was going to do anything anyway.

In the car was me, my brother Droma, my girl "Jo" and Tom, when we saw Cuba right near my house. He pulled over and told us Vor and the whole DBI crew were hanging out in Golden Field of Crocheron, right near the parking lot and Vietnam memorial. If you read my first book this area should be familiar.

Given all the shit Tom had been taking from all of us, and Duel just a few minutes earlier, he declared "Take me in there!" referring to the park where Vor and his crewmates were hanging out.

As we were walking in, Droma reminded Tom that he didn't have to do anything because like Duel said earlier, it was a "toy dispute". I mean everyone took every opportunity to pour gasoline on this fire! This really got Tom fired up with us laughing at the hilarity of the whole situation.

None of us had ever met any of the DBI crew before with the exception of Cuba who knew Sean from High School. They were a couple years younger than us and our association with TMR made us a crew they tried to stay away from for the most part.

For that same reason, our association with TMR made my own crew a bit feared, even though we did a ton of dirt and handled business on our own, our association with the larger more famous crew kept people away from us.

As we walked into the park, we could immediately see them on one of the benches, there about 12 of them, guys and girls mixed, listening to music and drinking beers. We walked in and they could see us coming, so the music was turned down. As is often the case when rivals enter a yard where you are the conversation drops to a minimum and everyone sat on the top of the benched with their feet on the seat, kind of just waiting to see what we wanted.

I didn't know who any of them were but Tom did and he starts naming them to me as we approach. It was MF, Dead, Vor, Rune, Bobby and a few girls and others.

"What you gonna do?" I asked Tom which prompted him to run up to one kid on the back of the bench and scream "stand up!"

Assuming this was Vor we just watched it unfold. "Are you serious Tom?" said Vor, "It was just a fucking tag!"

"Step down!!!' Tom screamed again as he had his hands up in a boxing stance and moved a little closer. Not wanting him to get punched sitting down, MF pushed Vor off of the bench and into Tom and they began going at it.

Each wailing on each other in a barely structured brawl before Tom ripped the shirt off of Vor's body prompting his to scream "My stitches" as he winced in pain.

We could visibly see Vor had stitches on his back and at that point broke the fight up and made them shake hands declaring their beef settled. The music was put back on and they offered us some beers, which we accepted, and we all hung out until the break of dawn together and became the best of friends through the next two years. Funny the way those types of things work out, even Tom and Vor would bomb and piece side by side many times over the next summer.

DBI shared in my brother's and my geeky obsession with graffiti and the thrill of the whole thing. I still tell people to this day, DBI was a crew that would fight if needed, though it was rare that they had to. They weren't soft by any stretch, and they had this real, no-bullshit passion for graffiti. It was never about the image or status —like us, they loved the illegality, the hustle of racking, the rush of bombing, and piecing. Outsider opinions? Didn't even register.

Not long after, my crew and I flew down to Georgia, picked up my brother in a rental, and headed to Daytona Beach, Florida for spring break in '93. We had a routine: stopping at every hardware store along the way and racking up supplies from each one. We'd pull a "summer rack," wearing loose sweaters over belted shorts, so we could tuck five cans across our waist and hide them perfectly.

Droma and I would each grab five cans, and Tony and Paul, who weren't even really into painting, would get five each just to support the CWB stash. That's twenty cans per stop! On the way out, we'd ask the clerk, "Hey, you got any old Krylon Spray-paint colors in the back? Specifically 'Icy Grape'?"—knowing full well they didn't. And when they inevitably said no, we'd follow up with, "Alright, what's the next hardware or paint store nearby that might?" And like magic, they'd direct us to the next spot.

By the end of two days, we had almost a thousand cans packed in the trunk, floorboards covered. When we dropped my brother back off in Atlanta, we left him with the whole shitload of cans in his college apartment—his closet was stacked floor to ceiling!

Graduation rolled around and my dad drove down with a minivan to pick him up. Droma loaded the cans in while my dad watched, wide-eyed. He couldn't believe we were still at it, especially since my brother had just graduated from a top tech school, summa cum laude. But some habits just don't die.

That summer of '93 was one for the books. I was off bail, and we were piecing with DBI multiple times a week. They saw the stockpile we'd built up and started stepping up their own racking game to keep pace. That year, paint cans were everywhere.

THE PLAZA HOTEL

Back in the mid to later 1980s, one of my favorite places to be, even alone, was in a train tunnel underneath the Central Park Zoo and across the street from the Plaza Hotel. It was a little-known place, at least in the mid 1980s, where they park two B trains every night before the rush hour the next morning. They also parked JFK trains to the planes in there a little further back, but we rarely painted those because it would get buffed soon and would only ruin the rest of lay-up by bringing police around into those tunnels.

Given the location of the tunnels it was a safe neighborhood in a largely unsafe city, so it was someplace I felt safe being and always went with my brother, Kite or Tame, or by myself meeting up with writers I knew that also went there like Ven, Chama, Tekay, etc. I would see Smith and Sane in there, JA, Kase 2, you name it, over the years.

But I never became a clean trains writer, once trains were largely cleaned by 1989, and the B Line no longer had graffiti on it, I called it quits. The clean train movement just did not appeal to me the way seeing your name on a daily basis on the subway system you rode to school and work did.

Most writers that started in the late 1980s or early 1990s never had the opportunity to write on subways in the 1980s. Either they were too young or did not have the exposure. I wasn't any older than many of the local Bayside writers that never wrote on trains, the difference was I went to Bronx Science, which exposed me to trains every day, all day, and the desire to see my name on those trains became so strong it fueled me to find a way. Without seeing it like that I likely would never have been out of my area either.

Kids used to ask me to take them to hit trains in the early 1990s, which I refused because even if we would get over, the idea of painting just for a picture was not a thing, the train wasn't going to run. Often, we didn't even take pictures in the 1980s. Contrast that to today's IG world where everything is done solely for a picture with almost no real-life exposure on anything we do.

One night though it was Cuba, Sean, Droma and me and they really wanted to go paint trains. I figure why not? We were painting that night anyway, let's spice it up.

We did not spend any time preparing, I did not go to spots I knew of and check them out with no paint to see if they would be good. Something I often did in the 1980s. Like one time me and Gibson went to 14st on the L on Christmas day with nothing on us just to enter the lay-up and see if we could walk through the train and then come back out without any incident.

The advantage of this was even if you got grabbed by the police, you would only get a trespassing ticket, often not even a night in the system, although they did put me through the Tombs once for the same.

This process was known in graffiti as "Scoping out". Writers would often scope out spots they were going to paint before they carried out the act actual mission. A form of reconnaissance, like a military operation in a way.

But the impromptu night with Sean and my brother we just went in cold, no "scoping out" was done, no recon. We brought bookbags and about 8 cans each, planning to do two whole cars of simple straight letters, dusty side by side on each car. We went back to my favorite place. 57ᵗʰ street.

We parked a couple of blocks south behind the Essex House and Ritz Carlton Hotels and walked across into Central Park. Right where the street enters the park, about a hundred yards to the West is a dirty yellow hatch in a grass field, just about across Central Park South from the Ritz Carlton. It's still there today and often I walk by it and reminisce.

The hatch has this screw in nut that sits at one of the ends, its usually not fastened too tight, and if it is I usually kept a small wrench in my bag. This central park hatch was so easy because as I said, it's in the field, across from the Ritz behind the wall to the park, hidden from view of passing traffic and not too far from tree cover as well.

I unscrewed the bolt and pulled it up, it has a chain attached to it which on the underside is attached to the panic bar release of the hatch push bar. It works like the exit door to a movie theater somewhat. It's designed as an emergency escape from the tunnel in case of a train disaster, as well as a service portal. Every tunnel has them throughout New York City and you've walked past them a million times probably without even noticing. Most are in the middle of sidewalks.

Sometimes when you would get raided and rush out of a hatch, particularly during the day, if it was in the middle of a busy sidewalk and you flung it upward into the pedestrian traffic, people would be horrified as they watched you scramble out. Like I said most people don't even realize these doors are beneath their feet.

But going in, you pull up on the chain and it pulled/pushed the release handle below. Now, being a huge metal door, it is counterweighted to assist its operation, if you do not control it sometimes it will fly open.

Once we got the hatch open you could see the glow of incandescent bulbs coming up from the dark below. The stairwell is dimly lit, and in the dark park it glowed, quickly we stepped inside, took a quick look back and pulled it closed behind us.

The metal stairs here descended about 2 stories into a train tunnel with one track running in either direction separated by a wall. On the first story, or half story down, there is a landing that extends on a metal platform like a bridge out into the tunnel above the train on each track. If the train comes it will go under you by about 2 feet which is really cool, its loud and the platform bridge is metal grating that you can see through. We used to love to hang out here. You would have to step into the center though when the train first approaches though because the conductor could see you if you were standing above the track and would likely call the police.

We often took tags in this area, and you had to wait until the train passed heading east before jumping into the tunnel to walk to the layup. You always wanted to jump in behind a train, because they were spaced out by a few minutes at least and you knew that you would then have a few minute head start on the next train coming down the track.

The clearance in some of these tunnels is nonexistent, meaning there is none. If you get caught with nowhere to go you would be killed by the train, it's happened many times back then and many times since where unsuspecting graffiti writers get trapped and killed. I know writers personally killed in similar fashion. As I've mentioned before, I speak about these stories and times like they are fond childhood memories, but the stakes were extremely high.

We jumped into the tunnel behind the train walking as fast as we could without running. I may not have moved quite as fast back in the 1980s when I did this all of the time, but it had been about 5 years now since I've been here, so the adrenaline was high, and our pace reflected that. Of my three companions, my brother had been here twice with me before, so it was still exhilarating to him, but Sean and Cuba had never been in a tunnel before, and I assure you, jumping into a dimly lit tunnel behind a loudly passing train and following it is quite intimidating the first few times.

Our conversation was minimal now, we were focused like a paramilitary crew entering a bank heist in the middle of the night. Bags of paint on our backs and forging ahead into the unknown.

When entering the layup from this tunnel it comes up from below about 200 meters before it merges with tracks on the left that come from above. Straight ahead at this merge is the 57th street station, you can see the platforms illuminated in the distance.

The tracks that come from the left side above also head into the 57th street station but they are not operable tracks for a route, those tracks fork off from where you just came but at a higher level, they last for about a quarter of a mile before ending and turning into tunnels and rooms with no tracks under the central park zoo on the 5th Ave and 60th or so street area of the park. This is where the trains are parked for the 57th street layup.

Normally, at least 5 years ago when I was last here, you would climb up as the tracks merge and walk away from the 57th station ahead into these tracks where the trains were parked. And that's what we did. But something was not quite right this time. Normally you could see the dim tunnel lights from the bulbs every 20 or so feet lighting the way, but tonight the tunnel was pitch black. An ominous sign that something was not quite right. But still, we could see the red running lights from the two trains parked in the tunnel ahead, so we continued.

It was dark enough that we almost had to hold onto the wall so as not to trip on the tracks and climb up onto the narrow platform the ran along one side of each of the trains. Once up there we moved closer to the trains before hearing voices and seeing flashlights up ahead. We froze in our tracks and just looked on.

We could not tell what was going on, but we could tell those were not graffiti writers by the vests and multiple flashlights and the sounds of radios being used for communication. In a whisper we agree to turn back the way we came and leave with the closest of the people carrying the flashlights now being just 10 yards away now and walking in our direction.

We turned to head to the lower tunnel when Droma stepped on a lightbulb that was on the platform creating a loud explosion that echoed through the tunnel. All the flashlights were now upon us.

"Hey! Stop!" shouted one of the voices in a loud husky tone.

We jumped into the lower tunnel, now not even knowing when the next train was coming and just hauled ass back in the direction we came with the flashlights beaming behind us. We ran like it was a race and as we got to the stairs where we came in, we saw men standing in the tunnel there too, two of them. But the flashlight crew was behind us and far greater than two.

We kept running towards the two men and one of them outstretched his arm to tackle me as they others juked right and left and ran past. I was running full bore like an NFL running back and my momentum carried me through his outstretched arms, spinning him around and to the floor as I bolted forward behind my crewmates.

Having had played tackle football in a league a few years earlier, I immediately thought to myself "He blew the tackle!"

We ran as fast as we could, even stepping it up now because they physically are trying to apprehend us.
The next place we could get out was the 5th Ave train station which was about another 100 yards ahead. The whole group of men was behind us yelling and chasing. And then we saw the train lights entering the tunnel coming right for us!

But it all happened so fast, it never even dawned on me that the train would crush us, we just kept running towards it. Then I noticed the train was stopped halfway into the tunnel leaving the station.

The men behind us were workers and cops, and on radios, they radioed ahead to stop the train from coming because they were in the tunnel, simultaneously stopping the train from crushing us in our heat of the moment lack of judgement.

When the tunnel gets close to the station there is some clearance on the side of the train, not much but at least shoulder width or a little more. In the dark tunnel we could see the conductor watching us run towards the train, we could see passengers on the train looking into the tunnel at us, I glanced back as my crew was climbing up onto the end of the platform, the men with the flashlights were getting closer but still about 50 yards behind us.

By the time I ran past the front of the train only Cuba still hadn't made it onto the platform yet, he was climbing up when I ran up behind him. I put both my hands on his lower body and launched him upward to help him, and to get him out of my way before climbing up myself.

We ran through the station like villains through a few passengers that were still on the platform, up the stairs and out onto the street. We bolted across towards the Plaza Hotel, seeing transit police vehicles and MTA trucks up the street at the hatch we originally entered through. We ran up 5th Avenue and turn down 58th street, we put our bags in some piles of garbage and split into two and two and agreed to meet at 54th and 3rd in an hour before splitting off in different directions briskly walking.

We met up and got some drinks from a corner store before returning to our car and driving to pick up our bags from the garbage. We were brazen enough to drive down Central Park South where we saw the whole area lit up near the hatch we entered through many official vehicles now on the scene.

A few weeks later after telling this story to some of my city writer friends, Chino told me that Sento took a group of European writers there not long before we went. They did multiple whole cars on multiple occasions, the trains being clean at this time were a huge priority for the city. The layup was blazing hot with the police and MTA without us knowing.

We walked into that layup completely oblivious, but hey, we got away, we survived, and we moved onto our next adventure.

CHAPTER 15

COEXIST

In graffiti, the origins of the word "coexist" has a far more nefarious meaning than what is meant by the popular hippie bumper stickers and movement where it means to all live in harmony and not worry about what your neighbor is doing.

In graffiti the word was coexist used by an infamous graffiti villain in "The movie" in 1981. "The movie" for those not familiar with the culture or movement is titled "Style Wars" and was made by some very well respected yuppy photographers documenting the amazing graffiti culture and artwork spawning from the darkest depths of the late 1970s New York City into the 1980's. "The movie" as it became known was welcomed with open arms by the inner-city youth portrayed in the film and the overall graffiti culture itself. Mostly because many saw it as a way out and it legitimized what was a dark subculture with some good intentions.

There are many differing views on "The Movie" and "The Book", Also known as Subway Art, a partner piece to the movie both showcased some of the most amazing subway graffiti ever done. Almost all opinions about these media pieces are positive from within the culture and outside of the culture. But what both the movie and the book did, was alter the natural order and flow of what graffiti was in a very real sense.

Both of those media pieces started to be made around 1979-ish when graffiti as the NYC culture we know today was not even a decade old, and as a result people were painting "For Henry" which meant they were painting for the movie or the book, no longer just painting for whatever motivated them originally. And people that never met in real life now had met through Henry and were now painting trains together. Thus graffiti history and trains we saw were altered by the influence of outsiders and media attention.

It immediately changed the intent of the culture and split many of its participants. Some wanting to stay true to the dark violent inner city causes of graffiti in the first place, some not even aware really of the movie and just looking to become hood famous amongst your peers and not give a fuck about the real world.

This involved violence, theft of supplies from both stores and other writers, it involved most of all getting your name up on as many trains as possible, to "King" lines and be the most up, the most "Famous" in your neighborhood or city.

To other writers though it was more important for graffiti to be an art form and for the trains to look nice, which was always lip service anyway. Because almost all the artists that were busy focusing on making the outside of the trains an Art gallery were also heavily interested in doing "Insides" with markers and ink. And insides were arguably the most disgusting part of graffiti as viewed by the normal citizen and government. I mean us graffiti writers loved insides, but the view from the city was it was vandalism in the worst form.

When Henry was making the movie, the producers and him discussed that this movie cannot be made without an antagonist to the film's protagonists. Its Hollywood 101 and they decided this movie wasn't going to be viable without a true "Villain".

This conversation really took place, and today many graffiti writers, many of whom were not even born yet, have opinions about this villain and what graffiti was supposed to be based upon this Hollywoodized version of the story told in "The Movie".

But one thing was clear, there were two schools on graffiti in the early 1980's NYC as the movie depicts, but they were not so clear cut. The best piecing crews also loved to do throw ups and loved to go over other people's shit. It wasn't just the villain who started this, he was just good at it.

This villain was a dude up in the Bronx that wrote CAP MPC, in the Morris Park section. And a lot of the piecing writers depicted in the movie did many of their pieces down in Brooklyn, at the other end of the 2 and 5 train lines that also parked in the Bronx near Cap and his crewmates. This created a natural beef that would've existed no matter how many pieces pulled out of the Bronx, because train graffiti required space, and it wasn't as if once you painted a train all of the other writers in the city were going to leave it forever, someone was going over it, if for no other reason than they needed the space. Doesn't matter how beautiful it was.

The movie really played up this aspect of the story and focused on a graffiti war that involved CAP and many other writers at the time. In 1981 CAP said in the movie "There's two types of graffiti trying to coexist, but it ain't gonna work like that." (Paraphrased a little) He was referring to pieces and beautiful artwork being "allowed" by the laws of the street to just run for ever and that other people, namely him and his crew were more interested in using the space for throw ups and simple ways to show their names as many times as possible.

Extremely violent conflicts happened as a result, and he was right in a sense, there were two types of graffiti trying to coexist, and it did not work out that way.

Fast forward another decade to the birth of legal Street Art at large. Sure, there were some street artists back in the early 1980s but most of them still painted illegally. By the early 1990s the idea of permission graffiti became huge. Places that would overtly allow you to paint, or schools that would give you permission, etc. And again, there were some examples of this in the 1980s as well, but they were few and far between until the 1990s.

Even some places that might not have been legal still were turned a blind eye by law enforcement for the most part and people just started painting there in the daylight as if it was allowed. You would see things like "Reserved for SO AND SO" written on cleanly painted walls, which meant that a certain writer was given permission, many times by other writers, to reserve a spot to come paint at a day in the near future. You see this kind of thing all the time in Florida now at Art Basel Miami. In Wynwood the graffiti covered streets are covered with "Reserved for SO AND SO" writings as the event gets close.

I like to get to Art Basel a day or two early and do throw ups in a lot of these spots, because after all, graffiti, at its essence, at its core, is about writing your name exactly here. Exactly where you are not supposed to. And random artists would see me and attempt to correct me. "I'm sorry, you can't paint there."

"What do you mean?" I would respond. "I can paint anywhere I want." And with that response you have to be ready for the consequences, which for me in that situation never came. Sure, they would go over me when the writer got there and rebuffed the wall but sometimes that might be a day later or two days, and I would get the free run until then on a spot that is free from risk from law enforcement. After all, you think the police are going to arrest me for writing my name on a wall that is reserved for another writer. What government law am I breaking?

But that's now, back to the 1990s. Graffiti was still a real street thing for most writers. And once again we find ourselves with two types of graffiti trying to coexist. But this time it is illegal mentality street graffiti vs. permission and reserved spot graffiti. It's almost as if people were adding "rules" to graffiti now. Not official rules that are part of laws being enforced that we had to look out for, rules created by artists that wanted to control their own world. And it wasn't going to work like that this time either.

Back in the day, we'd play basketball at Bayside High School, sometimes till dawn. Oddly enough, the court was lit almost all night, right between the houses and the school. We'd often hang out in the park, drinking and doing other things, besides playing ball. Sometimes, teams would show up from Jamaica or other neighborhoods in the middle of the night. We'd put our best five guys against them—usually drunk or high—and it made for some memorable summer nights in New York City.

One night in spring 1994, Dead DBI would pull up there at 3am, I want to say he was coming from work but not really sure anymore if he did work that year or not. Many of us were going to FIT at this point and not working, either way though, "Hillcrest is all buffed!" he exclaimed. Referring to a popular piecing spot at a school in Jamiaca-ish Queens. It was largely a daytime spot at this point, the school yard consisted of several levels of concrete walls and handball courts and was entirely smashed with graffiti.

It was completely sealed off from the public view at nights and on weekends when the school was closed, and the gates locked. So, once you climbed over a rather tall fence and descended a long flight of stairs, you were free to do what you wanted. This is one of those grey area spots, not legal, but also not guarded for the most part.

Occasionally cops would come back there if too much of a mess was being made outside of graffiti, and it could get risky but for the most part the biggest problem was deciding who to go over if you wanted to paint there. And deciding who to go over comes with the previously mentioned consequences. Always does, and always potentially will, although in today's street art inspired communities it is much less likely for there to be actual fights over graffiti anymore.

Another common misconception by newer artists is that buffing the wall somehow erases that a writer had a piece or throw up in that spot. It doesn't, again, it never will but the likely hood of conflict grows less and less as time carries us further away from the old New York city era of graffiti.

The reason Dead DBI was so excited that it was buffed is because it never was. He was driving by it late that night and decided to park to jump the fence and see what was going on in there or what pieces where there, and much to his surprised the main wall was clean end to end.

We all reacted quickly, me and Droma always has a few dozen cans of paint in our trunk, Det RIS was there and he had some paint as did Cuba DBI, and Dead DBI. That was all we really needed to hear anyway; we went straight there at 3am.

When we arrived, we brought a few baseball bats with us and laid them in front of our feet at the wall. As we always did because there was no way in hell someone was ever going to walk into a schoolyard and take all our paint, getting robbed as a crew would be career ending, and something you were never going to let happen because that part of your reputation is as important as your name getting up in the first place.

The wall was indeed painted grey and clean, and in white spray paint you could see written "reserved for SO AND SO" in each of the spots along the wall, which might as well have said "reserved for US". Because at this point and still, in graffiti there is no reserved. That is street art talk, and we literally didn't even contemplate that kind of thing for a split second.

It wouldn't have mattered who the names were, they could have painted back over it, and even then, famous or not, depending on our mood we might have raised hell. Because those were the rules of graffiti, and in painting over someone or something you must be willing to accept the consequences of your actions which could, and often did, result in violence against you.

But street art was now trying to coexist as legal graffiti in the beginning, trying to legitimize itself from graffiti by doing away with some of the barbaric survival rules previous in place. And when I say rules, they were rules by default, the rules of the streets in general. Where you had the option to do anything at any time, there were no rules if you get what I am saying.

But here we are again where two types of graffiti were going to try to coexist, and it still wasn't going to work that way.

We painted like the wind that night, no prepared outlines, just adlibbing our feelings in the moment, painting straight through the night.

The wall read STANE, DROMA, DEAD, DET, KRI, with crews painted and the wall themed "Graff's Twilight". At one point six or seven older dudes came in there and just sat on the benched and watched us for an hour.

When they first came in, we all made sure we knew exactly where our bats were, the first few minutes of another crew approaching your crew in a dark isolated schoolyard is always tense, but after a while you can tell it was in the form of spectatorship and we continued, them eventually leaving.

We painted as the sun came up and snapped some quick pics of our wall before heading home at 6am to get some sleep, Cuba was already passed out on the concrete floor, we had to drag him out of there.

We woke up the next morning early, like 10am, only a few hours after parting ways when Duel RIS and Det showed up to my house and banged on my door to go see the wall in full daylight and get some better pics. Sean CWB also came with us.

At the street entrance to the schoolyard there is a tall fence to climb over, it is a double gate about 8 feet tall, that would be unlocked on school days and where students would enter for school. But on weekends it was locked, which is one of the reasons it became a daytime piecing spot as I said, it was closed off from the public and far out of sight.

After climbing the noisy fence, you find yourself at the top of a long staircase made of concrete descending into the back schoolyard, with the main school building, a large two or three story building, to the left.

If you are in this schoolyard painting or doing anything down there, you can hear the fence rattling and clanging as people are coming in, creating a situation where often people would run over to the steps looking up to see who is coming,

As we got to the top of the steps, a writer named Rush EGM, who we remotely knew through mutual friends, ran over to the bottom of the steps and saw us. "Oh my god!" He exclaimed. "You guys are not going to be happy!"

Obviously, someone was going over us, so we proceeded down the stairs and found some slightly younger street artist writers had already covered us up not even three hours after we left. For the sake of this story and to protect the privacy of those that transgressed, we will call them writer MMM and writer OOO.

MMM and OOO were the two that had buffed the wall the day before, writing their names and reserved on the buff. By the time we got here now they had a whole production outlined and filled mostly in with horses and backgrounds and pieces. They must have just missed us when we left at sunrise and started then.

I was at a loss for words, Rush and other kids in the school yard at the time were also kind of laughing but trying to stay out of it. Duel is looking at them and he turns to me and says "Yo! They are going over you!"

"Stop painting!!!" I screamed at them loudly. They looked down from the ladders they were on and didn't know what to do, there were four of them total, they had a box radio playing music rather loudly. Next to the radio was a baseball bat that they had brought, largely for the same reason why we bring one, except this situation happening right now is the reason they brought the bat.

"Stop fucking painting!!!" I screamed louder as one of them now realized this wasn't going to go away, he climbed down off the ladder. "You guys are done! I'm going over this shit right now, you are done!"

Duel sees their baseball bat near the kid climbing down off the ladder and runs to grab it, in one motion he swings the bat smashing the loudly playing radio into pieces, through the new silence he exclaims "Oh we armed now!"

People start arguing and yelling back and forth, us, them, until Duel smashes some of their cans "Everyone shut the fuck up! This is a stick up!" He says, as an eerie silence falls over the school yard. A few kids scamper out over a fence into some neighboring back yards, others run up the mains stairs out of view.

"You are leaving us all your paint" I said. "We are going to redo our wall with it, don't fucking go over us again!"

"Take your cameras and bookbags and get the fuck out of here!" I continued, as they gathered what was left of their pride and their ladders and headed up the stairs.

Once out of site you could hear one of them scream "Fuck!" at the top of his lungs in frustration. Frustration that their halfway done wall is getting gone over, frustration that they were publicly humiliated, frustration that they lost their paint.

We've all been there on the graffiti side, we've almost all had things not go our way and get punched in the face or lost a bookbag full of cans getting rushed. In this instance the street artists were spared the physical violence that existed in our world, instead they just caught a glimpse of it, which of the two, that is the better option, a painless lesson taught by the streets.

We immediately got to work repainting our wall, the second time around it was STANE, SEAN, SHONE IF, RUSH EGM, and SONIC BAD that painted for the next 7 hours. I would wind up doing the RUSH piece as well when he had to leave early.

On this day graffiti and street art collided head on, and it has happened many times since, and graffiti always wins because like MIN says in "the movie" ..."You can't get (Them) back ..." and also like CAP says in the movie, "there's two types of graffiti trying to coexist" ...

And still, it ain't gonna work like that.

Note: Please don't not show up on my Instagram page saying the names of the writers who learned this lesson if you have knowledge of the incident. There was no lingering beef forward and we remained on good terms in the future.

CHAPTER 16

TWENTY-FIVE HUNDRED CANS

By the fall of 1994, my crew and I had started our college journey at F.I.T. in NYC. When I say 'my crew,' I'm talking about my girl, Dead DBI, our friend Jhomy, and a few others, while my brother was just finishing at Georgia Tech. College life brought along a bunch of new interests that began to overshadow my passion for graffiti. Don't get me wrong, my love for graffiti hasn't faded — that's far from the case. But let's be honest, graffiti life is no walk in the park. It's a grind, something newer graffiti writers and street artists might not understand.

The darker side of graffiti—like the theft, conflicts, beefs, police chases, and arrests—adds both thrill and hardship to the art. It's a paradox that makes graffiti simultaneously incredible and terrible. I've mentioned this before, and I'll say it again: anyone who's truly been doing graffiti, in the most genuine sense, has at some point felt like graffiti was ruining their life.

That realization might come on yet another lock up in The Tombs in Manhattan, or after getting punched in the face unexpectedly by a writer you didn't know was there. It was and is just exhausting at times.

Now, with the broadening horizons that college offered and my desire to leave behind the serious charges and the last two chaotic years of tagging with the DBI crew and on my own, it felt right to turn the page.

By this time, we still had a rap group, and by late 1994, we were hitting the local gig scene and dropping demo tapes. I even got back into playing the drums, something I started doing with my brother and Trent back in the '80s.

As I got more involved in the NYC scene through college and maturing in adult life, I began playing with a well-known NYC band in legendary New York City clubs. The three brothers in that band felt like my own brothers, and they still do today.

There were other things grabbing my interests, and I wanted more out of life now. Eventually, I might realize that there was nothing better in life than my early days of graffiti and '80s New York, but I needed to see more of life to figure that out.

My brother would come home for his last time from college that summer and we would line up and paint one last wall together with the DBI crew, marking the end of my NYC graffiti. It would be about 7 years before I painted anything again and when I did that would be in Los Angeles where it all of started over a bit. But I wouldn't paint again in NYC until more than a decade after this 1994 wall.

Ironically as well, this wall, my last true era New York City graffiti, would be the first piece of "Permission" graffiti I ever did. It wasn't planned that way either. It would happen to be at Franklin K Lane School, a public school in the Queens/Brooklyn border area withing view of the elevated subway.

It was illegal to paint here, and our goal was to bring ladders and do a top to bottom theme wall on a huge graffiti covered wall on the property measuring approximately 20 feet tall by 50 feet wide. But to bring ladders and set up for 10 hours of painting we needed to know the cops would not come get us. We couldn't run and leave ladders that we borrowed behind. School was out that next week as well for Labor Day I think, so the timing was perfect.

We thought we'd try something new — going into the school to talk with the principal to see if he'd be open to letting us paint a mural there. Given that the schoolyard was already covered in graffiti, we figured it might just be possible to get a written permission. This was uncharted territory for us, but it seemed worth a shot.

I was hesitant to talk to the principal because I always came off as rougher around the edges than my brother, especially with my tattoos. These things made me feel self-conscious about dealing with the "real world." Most people don't know this, but tattoos were illegal in NYC until 1997, a leftover law from the AIDS epidemic and hepatitis scares in the 1970s. Back then, it was rare to see young people with tattoos and I still looked about 16.

My brother, my girl Jo, and our friend Jhomy were a good-looking innocent group and we thought they would have the best chance. They did not want to do it without me and talked me into coming, which I reluctantly did; We all agreed I would stand in the back and not speak.

Our theme was Jungle Book and we were going to paint a forest, a snake or two and the Jungle Boy swinging through the middle.

Armed with a sketch of what we wanted to paint, we got into the school and began looking for the principal's office. Which is a weird thing compared to today. Four early twenty-year-olds entering a school they did not go to and wandering the halls. We were spotted by the school guard who may have been an actual cop at the time and we simply told him we needed to speak with the principal and he casually walked us to the office where they said he would "Be right with us."

This was before school shootings were a thing. There may have been isolated incidents of shootings over beef, but the concept of mass shootings for the sake of killing people in schools was not an existent worry at this time. The way it should be.

We entered the meeting, politely introduced ourselves as Art Students at FIT and shook his hand. We proposed covering a good section of the main graffiti destroyed walls with a themed mural and showed him the sketch and the book we stole from the blockbuster DVD of the movie. He thought for a minute before nodding his head and saying "Why not!"

He proceeded to type up a very formal permission letter on the school stationary naming my brother and "His friends" with carte blanche permission to paint a mural in the school yard.

We couldn't believe it, something I have saved to this day.

Now it wasn't specifically decided that this would be the last thing we ever painted together in NYC for me and my brother with the DBI crew. It just turned out to be so. This wall would also turn out to be the last thing I ever painted with my brother period. But we did have about 500 cans left between all of us, me and my brother having the most with about 300 and we did want to use up a lot of them. It was winding down for us. A year earlier we painted that wall together with the DBI crew at Hillcrest and my brother titled the wall "Graff's Twilight."

It's been something in our heads and I think after a certain number of years most graffiti writers feel this way. I know Seen UA referenced the death of graffiti in some of his pieces. Some before we even started writing. And we declared graffiti dead long before many of today's writers started. A cycle that will continue into eternity, I am sure. However far away "eternity" is for humanity in general.

Life is sad in its cycles and with the inevitable passing of each chapter, although graffiti never left us really, at least in our hearts. I would make several comebacks many years apart over the next few decades, including a 500 can crushing of freight trains as recently as 2022. But the end of the original New York City chapter for me is especially hard to reconcile.

We shot a ton of video painting this wall at Franklin K. Lane, we had an edited recap on VHS tape that I watched for years. Somehow in my carelessness in leaving New York the tape has been lost or borrowed and not returned. I would pay serious money to see that footage again, us in our youth, our last New York City mission for almost 20 years.

We arrived that morning at 8am, ladders borrowed, and one rented from Home Depot, strapped to the top of my dad's Jeep Cherokee.

There would be about 12 of us there that day at any given time, but the core group of us from start to finish was the four of us on the main wall, Dead, Vor, Droma, and Myself. My girl Jo would come and go and Kri and Noyze who painted the wall next to us would arrive a couple hours later. Various other stopped by here and there including our friend Jhomy and her then boyfriend, MF DBI.

It was a long day for sure, for the first time also here we buffed the wall with roller paint before proceeding. Something I had never done. It was a large wall and by the time just this task was completed it was almost 11am. The sound of the elevated train passing several times per hour is a nostalgic New York thing I look back on fondly and miss.

We would paint, and goof around, and paint until 9pm that night. Around sunset at 6pm-ish we discussed maybe coming back to finish it the next day but this was new to us also. Piecing with permission and we were sure if we left it unfinished someone might go over it overnight. So, we drudged on exhausted.

Of course, we kept stopping to do the one thing the principle asked us not to do and that was do throw ups on the school building itself, which was also already covered in graffiti. But writers will be writers and at the end of the day he had no way to know we did that because it was already bombed.

By the time we were finished our legs were in agony, especially Dead and Myself who did our pieces and the crew pieces at the top, and the characters up on the ladders. Droma and Vor worked largely on the floor, still exhausted but they were spared to constant climbing up and down.

By 5pm onward we finished the wall with a crowd gathered watching, about 15-20 strangers watched. Some of them writers, some neighborhood residents. Some approached us and asked questions like "Do you have permission ..." others wanted to talk about graffiti, some knew of us, some didn't.

Officially we themed the wall "Concrete Jungle" referencing the jungle like aspects of growing up in New York City in the past decade through the 1980's into the early 1990's. We had all endured so much.

As I mentioned we never set out for this to be our last hurrah, but we had been reflecting on the past 2 years recently, as a group. Especially my brother and I who were always looking for a connection between our actions and motivations and the greater meaning of it all. DBI had similar connections to their own place in the world of graffiti and the time in New York City. One of the things that made our crews so compatible and best friends.

We had been inseparable for almost 2 years as a group after that fateful night when Tom fought Vor and introduced us all to one another. We would sit up all night almost every night discussing graffiti, life, music, etc. Playing chess and doing what most would call real nerd shit.

Dead and Myself would often play "Subway Art Trivia" where we would never have a copy of the book present, but we would come up with questions for each other like "On the page where the Rolio Dien car is, there is a tag visible at the end of that train, what is that tag?" and from memory we would almost always know everything about that book. That was just a made-up example of a question, but we used to get quite specific and be incredibly accurate.

We would finish the wall up by writing "Twenty-Five Hundred Cans to Crush" next to Dead's piece. We had been reflecting on this too recently and figured that over the last two years as a crew we used up close to 2500 cans, maybe exaggerated a bit but certainly over 1500, plus what we had left amongst us, but it possibly could have been 2500. Either way that's what it felt like.

The sun symbolically set on New York Graffiti for me that night as we were doing this wall. A fitting end I think to what was an amazing run and the foundation of my entire life. With all that I would go on to accomplish in NYC before I left and in Los Angeles once I got here, graffiti still is probably the thing that I am the proudest of, as a vocation.

I am not proud of all the things I have done, not by any means, but the purity of the motivations and joy that we got from graffiti had a twisted sense of nobility to it, something that made all that went with it justifiable in a sense.

My biggest regrets are that I didn't capture more photos or videos of what would later become the most painfully nostalgic chapter of my life. I just wish I had realized back then how precious those days truly were—a sentiment we all eventually feel when looking back. Life's beauty often reveals itself when viewed through a different lens; in the moment, things can be tough, but the experiences we live through and survive shape us in many ways.

Of course, there are some harsh experiences we would have preferred to avoid.

There definitely was monster, a beast outside of ourselves to an extent. We were all seemingly good kids from somewhat loving families. Human nature left to its own accord will allow the beast in if we let it. Our chapter in New York City ended without much fanfare, my brother and I said goodbye to that house and that park that was central to most of our lives without even giving it a second thought for many decades.

Now all I do is think about it, about what went on. And I absolve New York City from being to blame, because once we got to Los Angeles at the end of the 1990s, the beast was there too, and it started over again with far more dire consequences for my crew.

Hard to believe after all of this, even with just the stories I shared in the two books, the worst was yet to come.

Franklin K. Lane 1994

FRANKLIN K. LANE HIGH SCHOOL

999 Jamaica Avenue
Brooklyn, New York 11208
(718) 647 - 2100
Fax (718) 235 - 4877

September 2, 1994

To whom it may concern:

████████████ and Friends have permission to paint a mural

on the back wall of Franklin K. Lane High School.

Yours truly,

Morton Damesek
Principal

MD:Lf

Franklin K. Lane 1994

FINAL THOUGHTS

I took a new job this year, the first job since 2005 where I had to commute to a location for working hours. There was a ten year stretch where I was an executive at a publicly traded company, starting not long after the birth of my son. And that job did require me to go into an office a couple times a month, in NYC, in Greensboro, work in Europe 6 or more times per year, etc. But it still wasn't the same thing.

I did not need to report to anyplace in particular on any given day. I came and went, and the perks were unreal. They essentially gave me a two bedroom and two bath apartment in a Doorman building in NYC, overlooking the east river, right on Sutton place. We had that apartment to use for about 6 years, and my son learned to walk there. He called it our New York House.

A friend of mine, Trent, a very good friend you know from these books, recently congratulated me for "Raising a New Yorker in Los Angeles", referring to my son, who if you didn't know any better you would assume he was a native New Yorker like me and his mother. I never really thought about the differences in being a New York native to what they call an Angelino, but in that compliment from my friend I realized that was something I cherished.

And the New York house as my son called it was instrumental to pulling that off. As if it was something

I had set out to accomplish, it wasn't but it was a pleasant result.

But my new job in 2023 was on location almost every day, from 8am until 4pm, with a very easy twenty five minute commute each way, it was a bit of a drive albeit a pleasant one. The job itself was project management for a rather large estate being rebuilt on a three-acre plot of land not far from Los Angeles.

The main house was about 7000 square feet and was gutted to the studs sometime before I was hired. The job had been stalled for about 6 months, stuck in the abyss of the planning department of the city of Santa Clarita and in their optimism that it would be started again soon, the owners and their designer hired me to run the construction.

But the delay was not yet over, so I was commuting to a large empty and mostly gutted house on a lonely and beautiful multi-acre plot of land, complete with a picturesque man-made lake and adjacent pool that looked like a water park. And I sat at a makeshift desk in this large, lonely structure 8 hours per day.

Alone for the most part except for a groundskeeper that I would occasionally see roaming the corners of the property. It was a lonely job which was good in a sense because everyone else involved were at the point of constant toxicity due to the delays and costs and idle nature. I would dread the incoming messages with questions asking me what I was working on, because they already knew the answer. What could I be working on?

There was no permit yet, they specifically told me they did not want me to get in touch with the city out of fear that I would frustrate that process even more. So, when they asked those questions via text, they knew there was nothing I really could be working on, nothing that was going to move this project along. And sure, there was some busy work from time to time or a delivery to the site that I had to process, but for the most part I sat here alone, much like Jack Nicholson in the Shinning. A keeper of the place, huge as it was, alone.

There is an In N Out Burger about 3 miles away from this jobsite, which was the closet store to here. The sign on the doors of the In N Out, all In N Outs, says the place opens at 10:30am. But in a steep tradition, In N Out actually opens at 10am, and is sort of something only "In"siders know. And before this job I had never really known this. I had pulled up to a drive-thru in the past at 10:15am and asked, "Are you open?" and they'd say yes and take my order. But I always just assumed that they happened to be open and never thought it was officially a thing. Until now.

There are people, at this location and I'm sure others, that queue up starting around 9:45 waiting to be let in. I never would've found myself with those people except that it was an excuse to get out of that house, and I eat a very light breakfast at 6:30 before I leave for work. So, by 9:30am I am ready to eat and use a restroom other than the porta potty at the jobsite.

There was an Asian man standing at the door the first time went. I put the window down "What time do they open" I asked. He turned to me and said "10 o'clock" very definitively. Making it now official in my mind. I parked my truck and walked up behind him as a biker in traditional biker garb and a very nice Harley was pulling up now, music blaring. People, In N Out workers, screamed hello to him.

Another car now too, a construction worker got out. There was indeed a queue, and upon going back another day I realized it was the same queue. A group of people from different walks of life that now sort of knew each other despite having very little interaction. They knew each other as other humans that liked what they liked, had the same habits.

The second day I went back I found a connection myself, and the third even more so. The Asian man was always first, always waiting when I got there. Every day he was ticket number 1. I was number 2, sometimes 3 or 4. And of course there were some other randoms each time.

The first time I sat to eat in a booth and the biker sat across from me in the next booth, facing me. Before he started to eat and I was about to eat, he toasted me with the burger he was holding in his hand before taking that bite. The way you might toast a total stranger in a bar with a newly poured drink. His was a 3x3, meaning 3 patties and three slices of cheese! He had that burger, fries, a shake and a soda in front of him. He was a large man, probably outweighing me by about one hundred pounds.

I had never had a "first off the grill" at In N Out before. Until then it was just ok to me, I could take it or leave it. But this single cheeseburger on this morning was different, it would make a believer in me. It was a single small patty freshly cooked on a clean hot grill, I added a whole slice of grilled onion, lettuce, tomato, and ketchup. I did not get French Fries but did get a soda. It was not a lot of food; the burger was dwarfed by the onion and the lettuce and tomato and single slice of cheese. It was delicious.

The bun was just slightly crunchy on the bottom rim where it sat on the grill for a moment to heat up as they cooked the rest. This is what everyone loved about this place. This is what these people here every morning loved about this place.

Besides the burger, and after only three visits, I found more than what I came for, which was a clean toilet and a reason to get out of that lonely house. I found an inexpensive truly delicious morsel of food in a world where those are few and far between. But more than that, in the familiar faces and in the familiar routine, I found a sense of belonging. Something I really needed at this time in my life.

I wanted to write this follow up book to my teenage journal debut, but I was having a problem, I just wasn't inspired to do so. Did the world need another book of tales of the dark side of humanity and a dark city where we grew up, probably. But more than that, would it have helped with my own redemption to add more fuel to that fire still not realizing a greater connection between myself and who we were growing up? No, it wouldn't have, it and I was missing something. Something believe it or not I found in this In N Out burger on these fateful mornings.

I needed inspiration, a tie back to the humanity, a way to humanize stories otherwise not humanize-able in some ways. Certainly, by today's standards.

In 1987, my friend Kite TMR, Jimmy Tame CWB, and myself were walking through the Village at about 10pm on a Friday night heading to meet up with Chino BYI and his boys for a night of mischief.

Many nights back then started off just like this. Going out, but not going anyplace in particular. Meeting up with others like us looking for mischief and worse to get into. These days it seems like you might set out for a night at a club or a party and maybe something happens, but back then we set out to nowhere, only looking for something to happen.

"It's 10pm do you know where your children are?" was a message that aired on TV channels every night reminding our parents to know where we were, because otherwise they might forget they had children. And true to its question, our parents had no idea where we were as we walked down a street behind 8th, heading towards Grays Papaya.

The Village was alive at this time on a weekend night, or any night for that matter. Walking from the double R train station beneath up onto Broadway was absolutely invigorating, exciting. The faces, all walks of life, the night was just getting started for most, for others it was the end of a long day. Traffic and yellow cabs raced from light to light as we crossed. A yellow cab was pulled over on the side street we were entering, and the driver was out of the car, there was some sort of commotion.

You see videos of this all the time now, an Uber driver with a passenger refusing to get out of his car and berating the driver in some way. The driver filming him and threatening to call the police. Even when the police come, there are no arrests, no justice is ever served for that Uber driver, the police just get the unruly troublemaking passenger out and let them go on their way.

But back in 1987 is not now, not modern day, in many ways it resembled the wild west more than it did today's world. The driver turned to the three of us as we walked past, he held out a twenty-dollar bill, a small-faced Andrew Jackson worth a lot more than it is today.

"This is yours if you get this asshole out of my cab!" he exclaimed. Without hesitation I grabbed the twenty, Kite opened the back door on the street side, the guy scampered towards the sidewalk door where me and Jimmy Tame were waiting. He scampered back towards Kite who got a hold of his hair and yanked him out onto the street.

In a series of kicks and stomps and punches from the three of us, justice was served. The cab driver smiled, satisfied with the result, he thanked us. He thanked us as if we performed a service and in many ways we did. The battered troublemaker gathered his things and wits and disappeared down the street. It was indeed a different world.

Is that story humanize-able? Are street justice and the laws of nature humanize-able? Surely, we acted like beasts. But was there a victim? That bully was refusing to get out of this guy's cab because he had the upper hand, the cab driver was feeble, but not mentally. He had the will to fight back and the wherewithal to devise a plan and when he saw three street kids walking by, he acted on that plan.

What were we supposed to do? I already said we were out to find mischief, we weren't going anyplace in particular, we were on those streets looking for exactly this kind of adventure.

Reflecting on this story, in this In N Out Burger on this morning, as I ate and felt content, I decided that we were redeemable, that story itself is a story of redemption. We didn't beat that man any more than necessary to send the exact message that cab driver wanted to send. The message he was entitled to send. We were messengers in a world we did not create, we were often the recipients of unpleasant similar messages ourselves.

Today I think that is referred to on the internet as "Fuck around and find out". We both found out growing up and helped others find out, and with that I hope you enjoyed the pages of this book. Some stories more innocent than others, some silly tales, but all of them bullshit, 100% fabrications of the minds of mad children growing up in the 1980s and 1990s.

And was there really a beast or was it just us?

I still have no idea.

ABOUT THE AUTHOR

Chris is a father, husband, artist and author currently living in Los Angeles. He has had several screenplays optioned and is in the process of completing another novel. He has been keeping journals and writing prose since college and still has many more volumes of stories to share.

Rest in Peace to my Mom and Dad, Mark Broderick (MB), and Tommy D., not a day goes by...

Thank you for reading!

www.ingramcontent.com/pod-product-compliance
Lightning Source LLC
Chambersburg PA
CBHW022027240626

47154CB00007B/2300